T0196769

ORTATROX

THE GREATEST GIFT

DONALD E. HORN

authorHOUSE®

AuthorHouse™
1663 Liberty Drive
Bloomington, IN 47403
www.authorhouse.com
Phone: 1 (800) 839-8640

© *2017 DONALD E. HORN. All rights reserved.*

No part of this book may be reproduced, stored in a retrieval system, or
transmitted by any means without the written permission of the author.

Published by AuthorHouse 07/13/2017

ISBN: 978-1-5246-9963-5 (sc)
ISBN: 978-1-5246-9962-8 (e)

Library of Congress Control Number: 2017910834

Print information available on the last page.

Any people depicted in stock imagery provided by Thinkstock are models,
and such images are being used for illustrative purposes only.
Certain stock imagery © *Thinkstock.*

This book is printed on acid-free paper.

Because of the dynamic nature of the Internet, any web addresses or links contained in
this book may have changed since publication and may no longer be valid. The views
expressed in this work are solely those of the author and do not necessarily reflect the
views of the publisher, and the publisher hereby disclaims any responsibility for them.

INTRODUCTION

The story that you about to read could one day come true. Unexplained things are, always being discovered. Many people constantly talk about being abducted by aliens. Some people have indeed disappeared without a trace and were never heard from ever again.

The Government doesn't like the public talking about this type of thing. Because they are afraid of many people panicking and going off the deep end. So, they try to cover it up the best way that they can. But, they can not stop all of the leaks from within their own system.

The story takes place high up in the Rocky Mountain Range, in the state of Oregon. If you don't believe that some things just don't exist, wait until you have read this book. The most unusual things have come to light. Could it be fact or fiction? You be the judge. For even myself have seen some things that should have never been possible.

CHAPTER *One*

While I am walking through the mountain forest, everything is so green with brilliant colors with different shades. As I look around myself, I see so many things. To my right, I have a rigid cliff towering over forty feet straight up. With ferns growing on little ledges. In several places along the cliff, I can see moss with water dripping off into a small pool at the bottom. To my left, I see trees, ferns, and flowers growing among the tall grass. Behind me, I can see the path that I have walked a long. Look how far downhill it goes! While in front of me, is still unknown, since I cannot see over the top?

As I look carefully, I can see a mist creeping down the path towards me. Slowly creeping along about one foot every thirty minutes. I must get to the top before I can take a rest break. So that my next leg of the journey will not be so difficult to handle. I sat down to rest about ten yards from the top. The mist is three feet away. The temperature has dropped a few degrees. The cool air had put me to sleep. I woke up about two hours later and found that I was completely surrounded by the mist. I could feel the dampness on my face and clothes. The mist was so thick, that I could not see three feet in front of me. It was as if the whole world had just disappeared, leaving me all alone.

The mist feels so nice and cool, on this hot summer day in mid august. The farther that I walk, the cooler that it seems to get. Luckily, for me, I had put some extra clothes and a jacket in my backpack. The temperature seems to have dropped about twenty degrees and now I am starting to get cold. Therefore, I took off my backpack, took out my jacket, and put it on. The mist is now getting thicker by the minute and I am having a hard time trying to see. Therefore, I picked up a stick that

I had just stumbled over to use as a prod. This is so that I do not walk into or off a cliff, or even fall into a deep ravine. The mountains can be so dangerous if you do not know what you are doing.

The many sounds of the forest that I heard earlier, has vanished. Everything is so completely quiet now. As though I had stepped through a time portal, I can't even hear any cricket's chirping. Like you normally would when it gets cool out,. I can feel the steep slope of the mountain path tapering off as I walk along. It should not take me too long to get to the top, if I am careful. I sure would not want to walk off or into a cliff.

Woe! I felt my stick hit something. Oh, it is just a huge log. I will just climb over it. Even though I have no idea of what is on the other side. Man, oh man! What a huge log this is! It must have been lying here for a few years. I can see parts of it missing and it seems to crumble beneath my hands. I think that I had better check the ground before I step off this log. That is funny; I cannot seem to find the ground. What has happened to it? I had better try to find some ground to walk on. I think that if I head towards the cliff, I just may find solid ground to walk on. Counting my steps, since I cannot see at all I finally found some ground to walk on. Now I check every step very carefully.

It's starting to get warm and it's getting easier to see now. That is not right, it should not even be getting warm. I want to find out where the mist is coming from. Therefore, I turned around and headed back for the spot where the ground that seemed to of disappeared. This must be the spot, I said to myself. It sure was. My stick did not hit anything. I wanted to see how big this hole actually was. I walked back over to the log. Checking each step very carefully as I went along. After I made it back to the log, I decided to see how big the hole actually was. I counted my steps as I checked the ground so that I did not fall in. I counted about forty yards around. That made the hole about sixty feet across. I am at least twenty feet away from the log. Let's find out how deep this is. I felt around for a rock of a descent size. I dropped it down into the hole. It was almost as big as a baseball. I could not hear a thing. I stood there for about five minutes trying to listen for the rock to hit the bottom. However, I heard nothing at all. I want to check this out some more. This might be a deep pit with mud in the bottom of it. However, I am not quite sure that this is the case. The mist seems to be cool as I hold my hand out over the edge of the pit. It seems to be coming up out of there. Where can it be coming from?

Did I remember to bring my tricks of a back packer's trade? Yes I did. I am sure glad of that. Now I can investigate this more easily. Where is that big ball of string? Here it is, hiding beneath my underwear. Man, what a strange place for that to be. I wonder if it is going to be strong enough. It must be. I cannot even break it. Ouch. My hand is a little bit sore from trying to break it. If I remember correctly, I should have over two thousand feet of string. I carry a lot of it, since I never know what I will need it for. And it's very thin too. Now I need something to tie onto the end of it. This will work just fine. A nice piece of rock about four or five inches square and rectangular. I wrapped it a half dozen times to make sure that the string does not slip off. Over the edge you go. I better sit down and do this as I unwind it. There is no telling how long this will take. I think that I had better take notes on this.

August 15th, 2025; 2pm. Normal temperature was about 85 degrees. Right now, the temperature feels like it may be about 70 degrees. Right above the pit, it feels even cooler yet. I cannot hear any kind of sound coming from anywhere. It has been about twenty minutes and I am still unwinding the string. I thought that I would have hit the bottom by now. However, I was wrong.

3pm; I have let out half of the string that I have and have not hit the bottom yet. That makes it about one thousand feet deep so far. Moreover, I am still going. I was letting out about 350 feet every twenty minutes. Where is the bottom? I have no clue. I have never seen anything like this in my entire life. I wonder how deep this really is.

3:30pm only 250 feet of string left and still no sign. Is there a bottom to this? On the other hand, does it go on forever?

4:18 pm; I finally hit the bottom of whatever this thing is, and I only have about twenty feet of string left. That makes it about 1,980 feet deep. That is the deepest pit that I have ever heard of. It sounds impossible, but I do have proof. I hope it does not take me very long to bring it back up.

4:45 pm; the string is showing a sign of moisture in which I do not like. If it gets to wet, it could stretch and break.

5:00pm; still pulling up the string. Now it is showing signs of great moisture. My hands are getting quite wet from the string. It is also getting more difficult to bring it back up. Nevertheless, I am not going to give up.

5:20pm; I finally finished pulling up the rock. I studied it carefully. The sides are very wet and I see something on the bottom of the rock. What is this? It seems to be some kind of slime. What is down there that could produce this type of slime? I better put this rock in a plastic bag and take it with me. I put the rock in the plastic bag, being careful not to touch it in any way.

Now according to my map, the road should be no more than one mile away from here, in the same direction that I was originally heading in. That should be Hwy. 22 North. That means that I should be going west. The mist was coming at me. Then I almost walked out of it. I stopped and turned around back to here. I am continuing on my journey towards the road.

Departure time is 6pm. It took some time to pack everything back up. Still using my stick, I headed out. I have been walking for a while and covered about half a mile. The mist is finally gone. Once again, I can see all around myself. Now I can hear the sounds that the birds are making off in the distance. I am stopping here for a few minutes to rest. I looked back to where I can see the mist. Woe! That is thick! It seems to swallow up everything in its path. I will rest here for about half an hour. Then I will continue towards the road. It sure has been a very long day.

It is 7pm and I finally made it to the road. I had better mark off a spot that can easily be found. Well, there are enough rocks here to work with. I guess that I will just have to make an arrow pointing the way. It is going to be dark soon, I think that I better had make camp off on the side of the road for tonight. I suppose that I am hundreds of miles away from any small town. Tomorrow I will find out for sure where I am. I am so glad that I brought these nuts along with me. There is no telling how long I will be out here. The time that I spend out here tonight, I will make good use of. It is time for me to build a fire, so that I will stay warm for a while. It tends to get a bit chilly up here in the mountains at night. To bad that there is not any one, I could talk to out here. It definitely would be nice to have some company. Six hours has gone by and I have not seen one car. This highway must be a lonely one. Maybe someone will come by tomorrow. I had better get some sleep while I can. I have a very long day ahead of me tomorrow.

It is 6:30 am and I woke up to the chattering of birds in the trees. I ate my breakfast and broke camp. My main objective is to get to the local sheriff's office to try to find out if there are any scientists in these parts. If there are, I must go see them to find out what this slime really is. Of course, they will want to know where I got it. Nevertheless, I will keep this a secret. That reminds me; I better look at my specimen and see what it looks like. I could not really tell in that thick mist. It just blocked out to much light. Right now, the light is perfect for <u>examining</u> things up close. Well now, this is very strange. The slime is clear. However, the string on the rock is blue. Half of the rock is Black Crystallite and the other half with the slime is a rustic orange color. Why did it change like that? This I must also find an answer for. There is no telling what this stuff is, or even if it is dangerous to living things.

I still have not seen any traffic. I better head on out before in search of a town. I am going north on 22 and the town is suppose to be only five miles from here. How big it is, I do not know.

8:15 am; I came up to a sign only a couple hundred yards from the marker. I had better mark both sides of the road to show how far away I am. This way I will know that I am close and that I should start looking for the arrow. It sure is a beautiful day out here today. Sure is perfect for taking a long walk. So far, it does not seem to be too awfully warm. There are only a few clouds scattered about in the sky. Which will give me a little shade every now and then. I will certainly enjoy that. Well its 9:30 am and I came up to a sign that read, Idanha 1 mile, population 2,500. Therefore, I pushed on even though I was getting tired. I made it to the town in 20 minutes. Sure is a quiet town. Not much of anything going on from what I can see. Ah, there is the Sheriff's office. I wonder if anyone is home. The door was unlocked. I walked right on in uninvited.

"Hello, is there anyone here?" A voice came from around the comer. "Just a minute." It was the sheriff. He was on the phone talking with someone. I listened in on his conversation to pass my time by while I was waiting.

"Yes sir Mayor." "I'll bring my wife over for dinner tonight." "What time is dinner?" "7:00 pm." "Okay, we will be there about 6 o'clock." "Then we can go over some of these proposals that I have been working on." "I certainly want to bring more business to our community." "All right, I've got to go now." "I have someone standing in front of me, waiting to speak with me." "You have a good day to Mayor." "Bye." Click, he hung up the phone.

The Sheriff was about in his late 50's with a few wrinkles on his face. His hair was slightly gray. His uniform was blue with a black stripe going down the side of each leg. His badge was a golden seven, pointed star with a blue center, with white lettering.

"What can I do for young man?" "Sheriff, I need to know if there is a laboratory anywhere in these parts." "Yes there is." "Why do you ask?" "Well, I have important business to discuss with the lab tech." "Can you tell me how to get there and how far away it is?" "What kind of business?" "I can't tell you that Sheriff." "It is privileged information and I can't discuss it with you." "I hope you understand." "Oh yes, I understand quite well." "You know, it's not everyday that someone walks in and asks for the lab." "The lab is about fifteen miles north on route 22." "Just on this side of the town of Detroit." "That's a good name for a town." "It sure is." "Is there any local bus or other transportation that goes between the two towns Sheriff?" "No, I'm terribly sorry that there is not." "We just aren't large enough or busy enough for that." "Matter of fact, you are the first stranger through here in about three months now." "Can I have the phone number so I can call the lab?" "Sure." "The number is 779-2318." "The area code is the same." "You can use my phone." "Thank you very much Sheriff." I picked up the phone and dialed the number that he gave me. It is ringing, someone answers. "Hello." "Is this the lab?" "Great!" "I have something of great importance to discuss with you." "But I don't have any way to get there." "Can you send someone to pick me up?" "Yes I understand that you are quite busy." "But this can't wait." "No, I don't want him to bring me there." "The less people who know anything about this, the better I will feel." "Thank you." "Who do I look for?" "A white van with a Blue Eagle on the door that says Blue Eagle Labs Inc. underneath." "Okay." "About how long before it gets here?" "Twenty-five minutes." "That will work out just fine." "I'm at the Sheriff's office in Idanha." "Thanks and I will see you when I get there." Click, I hung up the phone.

"Thank you again Sheriff." "You are welcome." "Is there a pop machine close by so I can get a soda?" "No there is not." "But I do keep some Coca Cola in the refrigerator right over there." "Just help yourself." "How much do I owe you Sheriff?" "Nothing at all." "It's on the way." "Thanks!" "You are a pretty nice guy, Sheriff." "Anytime."

While I was having my soda, I decided to ask the sheriff a few questions. "Tell me Sheriff...," "Call me Bill," as he interrupted. "Okay Bill." "Has there been any strange or weird things happening in these parts?" "Why do you ask?" "It is that I am very curious about this area." "Well, I have seen things that don't add up." "You might say that something has been going on." "What is that Sheriff?" "The animals have been disappearing, little by little." "What kind of animals?" "Oh, Possums, Squirrel, and Raccoons." "That's not so unusual." "Is it Bill?" "Yes it is." "They used to be so plentiful around here." "But now they're almost gone." "Is that it Bill?" "So far it is." "Except that some shiny stuff was seen near some of the remains of a squirrel." "Really?" "Oh yes indeed." "Did you get a sample?" "No, I didn't happen to think that it was that important at the time." "Now it would be too late to get one." "Why do you say that Bill?" "It just seems to vanish after a few days." "You are joking." "No I'm not young man." "Is there anything else Bill?" "Oh yes there is." "The stuff turns things different colors." "Cool." "Well Bill, I want to thank you for the information." "It was very helpful." "It is 10:45 and my ride should be here at any time." "I'm glad to have been of some service to you." "I hope that it helps you with your quest." "You have a good day now." "You hear?" "Sure thing Bill and you do the same." "Thanks and good luck."

I went outside and sat down on the steps. I did not have to wait for long. Before I knew it, the van showed up. I got in the van. "Your here to pick me up?" "Good." "Fasten your seatbelt so we can be on our way." "Sure thing driver."

It seemed like the trip only lasted ten minutes. Because I was busy looking around for unusual things along side of the road. The van pulled up to a long but old building. "We are here and the man you want to see is through the third door on your right." "Thank you very much driver." I got out of the van and walked up the sidewalk to the door.

Opened it and entered the building. I then proceeded down the hall to the third door on my right. I opened the door, walked in and sat down at a desk where a man was sitting.

"Well now." "You must be the person I spoke to on the phone earlier." "Yes I am." "Show me what you have that is so important." "This is it." "A rock?" As he boldly laughed at me. "It's not the rock." "It is what's on the rock." "I stumbled upon a very thick mist." "In the middle of the mist is a very deep pit." "The mist seems to be coming up out of the pit." "A very cool mist at that." "Take a real close look at the rock." "Do you see what is on the rock and how it has changed the rock altogether?" "Ah yes." "I see it now." "Yes that is very peculiar." "Where did you get this sample at?" I got it up in the mountains about twenty-five miles from here." "How long have you had this rock?" "I picked it up yesterday late afternoon." "I got here as quick as I possibly could." "The Sheriff in Idanha said that it disappears after a few days." "It's a good thing that you got this sample here, when you did." "It will give me a little extra time to work on it." "Ugh, sir, whatever you do, don't touch it with your hands." "Why not?" "It seems to be highly corrosive." "That is a good piece of news to know." "Thank you for telling me." "Now I will use the tongs instead of touching the string." "But why didn't it eat through the plastic bag?" "It is possible that it might only be corrosive to living things and materials." "Does that make sense to you doctor?" "Yes, yes, that is very possible indeed." "I had an old professor at the university where 1 studied." "He told me not to believe in everything that is supposed to be." "Because there are things that don't make any sense in the beginning, but after the fact." "I've got to start on this right now." "There are many tests that need to be done on this rock." "I may have to bring in a few colleagues to assist me." "I want you to come along to the lab." "You can finish answering my questions there."

We went down a long corridor, passing several doors along the way. We came up to what looked like a single bookcase. He pulled a book from the shelf, reached in, and pushed a button on the backside of the shelf. The bookcase swung open. Right before us was a hidden elevator. We stepped in and pulled the bookcase closed. The elevator started going down. I counted the levels as we descended. I counted fifteen levels when the elevator finally came to a stop. "Why are we so deep underground doctor?" "We don't want any organisms escaping to the surface." "This particular level is the most extreme level we have." "If anything gets loose in here, an Automatic Laser Tracker will start up." "It will follow anything large or small and eliminate it completely." "It won't leave any traces of living material at all behind to be discovered."

"Can I feel safe down here?" "Or should I get my tail out of here?" "You are as safe as a bug in a rug." "Things can't go wrong without an accident." "Do you want me to stage an accident, so you can see for yourself?" "No, no." "I'll take your word for it." "I trust in what you say." "Terrific!" "Let me get started then." "I will call a few of my colleagues in to assist me." "You can wait in there, as he pointed to a small room to my left. "Everything that you need is already there." "Including cable television." "Sometimes we get to tired to drive ourselves home and go in there to relax." I went over to the small room and went in to look around. "Seems like you people thought of everything." "You even have the kitchen sink in here." "Yes we like to think that we are at home here." "When we come across things like this, we tend to spend a lot of time here." "Many a time we spend long hours here trying to solve the answer to some of these riddles." "Enough talk." "It's time for me to get to work before this stuff disappears on me."

He took the rock out of the bag with the tongs and placed it on a glass tray. He took a drop of the substance and put it on a slide. He then put the slide under the Electron Microscope and turned on the viewer so that he could get a closer look at the substance. What he had seen disturbed him very much. He had never seen such a structure, like this one had. It consisted of fourteen different molecules. All of them he could not identify at all. This was a completely new substance to him. He then put a drop in several glass trays that they used for testing specimens. Then he added a different chemical to each and every one of the samples. Every one had changed into something else. They all had different colors and textures.

"You said that you got this from a pit?" "Yes I did?" "We need to find out more about this substance." "I have never seen anything like it before." "But first I must make a call to my colleagues." He went over to the phone and placed the call. He was on the phone for about fifteen minutes talking with them. Then he hung up the phone and went back to work on the substance. He took a drop from each of the trays and put them on slides. Then he placed them under the microscope, one at a time. After he completed that, he typed the information into the computer for the others to refer to when they get here. "You might want to try some skin and blood samples on the slime." "Why do you say that?" "The Sheriff and I had a very long discussion about this slime." "He told me that some of the animals were disappearing from the area." "That is very interesting." "Then I will try that."

He took out two more glass trays from the cabinet and put a drop of slime in each one. The he added a drop of blood to the first one and waited to see what it did. He took a drop of that, put it on a slide and placed it under the microscope. After he completed that, he recorded the results into the computer. The skin sample he did a little differently. He put a piece of skin right onto the slide, set it under the microscope and placed a drop of the slime right onto it. He typed the results of that into the computer as he watched. There was one more thing that he wanted to try. He took a bottle of Hydrochloric Acid from the shelf and carefully poured some into a glass tray. To that, he added a drop of the slime. The acid had no affect on the slime. This had puzzled him greatly. He then proceeded to put an Electrode to one that had a drop of water added to it. At first I could see it grow, doubling in size. Then suddenly it started to smoke and eventually disappeared without a trace. The one with the sugar water added to it, had turned into a Yellow Crystallite. You could see right through it. How extraordinary and beautiful it had looked. It also had a very unusual shape to it. It had twelve different sides. He then documented everything that he did, right into the computer. He was working as fast as he possibly could without causing an accident.

The one with the drop of blood in it also turned into a crystal. The color was very similar to a Ruby. The one with the skin had dissolved altogether. However, it had changed color too! This time the color was an Olive Green. Some of the other samples had amazingly good results. Then he noticed that the acid did do something. It should not have turned out as it did. It should have been completely eaten up by the acid. Nevertheless, it did not. It turned into a thick rubbery gel. It almost became a solid. Nevertheless, it could still be molded. The toxic odor was completely gone. So many things were happening.

He scratched his head from time to time. Trying to figure this out. Nevertheless, he was very much stumped. He took the rest of the slime sample and put it into a tight glass container to prevent it from being lost or spilled. He then put it into the refrigerator to try to preserve the structure of the slime. He covered all of the samples and placed them in the refrigerator.

He received a phone call that his colleagues would be here in ten minutes, from what I could hear. He walked over to a box that was hung on the wall. He took a key out of his pocket, unlocked the box and opened it up. Inside the box was a blue phone. He picked it up, pushed a button and was immediately connected. He was talking to the Chief of Staff in the military. He told him that he had stumbled across a substance that he could not identify and that he had called in his team. But he also wanted to put together a much larger team. He also wanted another team to go with him to investigate the area where the substance was found. He asked the chief how long it would take them to get here. The chief's answer was that they would be here in about three hours and for us to sit tight. He said that he would wait for them to arrive. He also told the chief that he needed equipment that is more advanced for both, the lab and in the field. The chief said that he would have what he needs. He hung up the phone and locked up the box.

He walked over to me. "We have to sit and wait for everyone else to arrive." "We might as well have a seat and get comfortable." "When they get here, there is no telling when we'll get any rest." "Is there anything else you can tell me about the surrounding area where you picked up the slime?" "Every little detail is very important." "No matter how crazy it may sound." "Some things never make any sense at first, but do in the end." "Well the whole area was surrounded by a cool mist." "So thick, that you could hardly see at all." "The closer that I got to the source, the cooler it got." "The sun couldn't be seen any longer due to the mist being so thick." "It was like it was almost getting dark out." "But I could still see some light." "You know how it gets when we have a very heavy fog sitting over us." "It is much like that." "There was a lot of moisture near the hole." "And there's a log on one side of the hole." "It was very large and it crumbled from beneath me." "There were no sounds from the animals, birds, or insects." "Usually you can hear them." "But not where I was." "There was a rocky ground surface to walk on at the spot." "It was almost like being in another time and place." "As far as anything else, I couldn't say at this time." "If I remember anything else, I will let you know." "You really can't see much of anything there." "You may be right." "There are some things in this world that just don't seem to belong." "But yet again, they are here." "Why?" "No one really knows." "There are still many new things being discovered on this planet of ours everyday." "We still have much to learn about this one before we can even think about going to another one." "But the government doesn't see it that way." "They seem to think that they can do it all at the same time." "One thing that our government seems to think is that our planet is rapidly running out of space to live." "But my theory is if we take and tear down some of these useless single homes, that we would have plenty of room for everyone to live." "There is no longer any need for people to own the land in which we live." "It is very true that the farmers can't hardly make a living anymore." "But that is due to the cause of the land being eaten up by the greedy land barrens." "They could take many of these old buildings and replace them with multi-floor buildings." "With several elevators in each and every one." "I am sure that the people would appreciate somewhere much nicer to live and help protect it from vandals." "Well that's enough of my ramblings." "There is much to do when they all arrive."

The first group had just arrived. They all gathered around the computer to study the results of the tests that had already been run. Each one had their own opinion about what this was. However, none of them actually knew. Then they went over to the refrigerator. They opened it up and took out the specimens to study. They were very astonished at what they saw. Because they have never seen anything react in the way that this substance does.

"Only one of you can go into the field along with us." "The rest of you will stay here and keep working with the military scientists." "I need for you to find out what this substance is and what its purpose is for." "I also need to know what it does and doesn't do." "Mike, you are the lead Geneticist here." "You will assist them as much as you can." "Dale, you are going with me into the field." They all agreed that this was a good decision. "Dale, come along with me." "We must get our equipment ready." "We need a portable lab with all kinds of slides and test tubes." "I also want to get our safety suits ready to go." "I don't want to take any chances out there." "You got it." "This man over here is responsible for bringing us this substance." "By the way, you never told me what your name is." "I know, you nor anyone else ever asked me." "My name is Eric Hymerman."

Eric is a mild mannered person. He is about six foot three inches tall. A rather slender built man. Weighing around two hundred pounds. He has brownish black hair, cut rather short. He is a highly educated man. Graduating from Yale College with high honors. He is about forty-five years old. "I have heard a lot about you." "You are the famous adventurer in this country." "From what I have read, you have found many unusual things." "One that I can recall is the lost city of our ancestors." "The tribe of the Yeti or Big Foot." "Yes I am." "I am quite proud of the work that I do, doctor." "Well it sure is a pleasure to have finally met you." "Thank you Dale." "I really appreciate the compliment." "Hey doctor." "What is your name?" "Eric, my name is John Kline." "I am a physicist." "Tony Anderson is a Biochemist and Mike Babcock is our lead Geneticist." "They will do everything in their power to come up with some answers for us." "We will always be in close contact with home base." "Without their help, we could end up in serious trouble." "We all will have the very best equipment at our disposal that the military has to offer." "Our job is to find the cause of this slime and how it has come to being here on our planet." "Or, at least, where it has derived from." "Sometimes nature has a very unique way of creating new things for us to discover." "And this may very well be one of them." "If no one has any questions, I want to get started on what I have already begun." "This slime only lasts a few days before it dissolves or evaporates." "Every minute is now crucial." "Find me some answers as quick as you possibly can." "Time is not on our side."

"John, I have a question for you." "What is Dale's last name?" "Or is it just Dale?"

"Oh no, Eric." "I am so sorry to the both of you." "This fine young man is Dale McCoy." Dale is a young man around the age of twenty-eight years old. He graduated in the top of his class. He went to the Penn State University. Dale has brown hair and green eyes. He stands about five foot six inches tall. His weight is about one hundred twenty five pounds. He has a slender build to him. He is a very quiet man. Who doesn't get around much with the women. However, he has been working on that problem.

John Kline is a well natured man, who takes his work very seriously. He does not take to kindly to people who tries to waste his time. He has been divorced from is wife now for about four years. He seems to miss her very much. Though, he doesn't talk about her at all. He stands about five foot nine inches tall. Around forty-eight years old. He has a well distinguished look about him. With a well up bringing. His hair is of a sandy brownish gray. His eyes are blue. He has a mustache that is cut short but very thick. It also matches his hair color. He wears his hair rather short, but it is very wavy.

About two hours has passed. They have their suits and lab equipment completely put together and ready to go. They are now waiting on the military to show up. John went over to the others to see how they were coming along with the project. So far, they have over 253 samples laid out on the tables. Each with a different substance added to the slime. Some of them have more than one compound put together. Nevertheless, they are drawing blanks. This substance has molecular properties that cannot be identified. Every time they add something to it, the molecular property changes to something else.

In which they also cannot identify. Some are very similar to substances that we have here on our planet. Nevertheless, are still very much different. Hope fully before long, they will come up with some kind of answer.

The phone rings and Doctor John Kline answers it. "Hello." "Yes this is Doctor John Kline." "Good, I'm glad to hear that." "Send them right on down." "By the way." "Who did they send?" "General E. Hawser." "Okay, _ will expect him shortly." Click, as he hangs up the phone. Five minutes later the General had arrived down on the fifteenth level with a group of men. Doctor Kline walks over to the General and greets him.

Hello Eugene." "It is good to see you again." "What do you have so far?" "We just have a whole lot of mysteries so far." "We have tried so many things and came up with nothing that we can even begin to explain." "Right now we don't even have a clue as to what this is supposed to be or do." "I think that we will find more answers out in the field." "All right so it is then." "Sergeant Hicks, get their equipment loaded up onto the trucks." "Yes sir General." He took three men and started to load up the elevator. Captain Johnson, you will get your team together and assist these men here." "Give them everything that they need." "If we don't have it on hand, then go ahead and order it." "Captain Miller, you will go with us." "Yes sir," they replied. Captain Johnson then carefully hand picked three dozen men to remain behind with him. Besides the four scientists that had already gone to work. It only took three hours to get all of the equipment that they were taking from down below loaded onto the four trucks. This was not even counting the vast equipment that they had already brought with them. They were ready for anything, especially the unknown. They had more equipment than you could ever imagine. They were even ready for a battle that might arise.

"Who is this man over there and what is he doing here on military property?" "Eugene, this is Eric Hymerman." "He is the one who brought this substance in and brought it to my attention that there was something out of the ordinary about it." "He told me all he could about this stuff." "But he never told me the where he found it." "Fine then tell us where you found it so we can get going." "With due respect sir, I will not tell you where it is." "But 1 will show you." "This is my find and I want the credit that goes along with it." "I can't take you along." "There is no telling what we will find." "Sorry sir but the only way that you will find out anything, is to take me along with you." "All right, all right." "I don't have time to play games." "But you are responsible for your own well being." "I can't expect my men to stick out their necks to protect you." "Don't worry sir; I have been all over this country and without anyone's protection." "I can protect myself." "Okay lets get going." "We still have lots to get done before sunset."

Everyone piled into the trucks and they headed on down the road. There were about twenty five trucks in all. Ten of them just to carry the vast equipment. The group of men that were left behind were unloading their equipment and setting up the radio. The trucks had reached the end of the two-mile long drive. "Which way do we go from here?" "General, we go south on route 22 through Idanha." "When we get to Idanha, we will have about another five miles to go." "I have marked a couple of areas that will show us when we are getting close to the area." "One is a marker on a road sign and the other is in the shape of an arrow, which points to the east." "Once we get there, the area is about one or two miles in." "That's a real good description of the area Eric." "Thank you very much sir."

The General then got on the radio and spoke to the Sergeant. "Sergeant Hicks, I want you to set up a small base camp in Idanha." "Make sure that your squad keeps anyone from following us." "Don't let anyone through, unless they have all of the proper orders in hand." "Yes sir, General Hawser." "I will get it done." We have been on the road for over thirty minutes. We had just come to the edge of the town of Idanha. It was still very quiet. I didn't see anyone on the streets. What could be going on here? Why are all of the people hiding? There were no answers for my questions, just many thoughts. As we were leaving town, Sergeant Hicks and his men broke off formation. They had pulled over to the Sheriff's Station and set up a roadblock. I guess that is where they will set up their post. "I hope no one gives them any trouble." "They can handle themselves quite well." "That is why I chose him for the job John."

Now there were only five more miles left. Then we might have to go on foot the rest of the way. We will see when we get there. The forest is leaping with life right here. We have passed a few deer along the way. There was a Hawk sitting on top of a telephone pole. "One more mile to go." "There's the marker on your left." "The arrow should be coming up very soon." "Start slowing down driver." "When you see the arrow, I want you to pull in and stop." "Yes sir General." We had finally come up to the spot that I had marked out. The entire fleet came to a halt. The General sent a dozen men south on 22. They went five miles to block off the road. Allowing access to absolutely no one.

The path was narrow and winding. The General had four of his men get out the two bulldozers that they had brought with them. They were to follow behind us and take out some of the trees. However, they were not to take out to many. He wanted to save the forest as much as they possibly could. The General seemed to be short and to the point about everything. Nevertheless, he was still a fair and just man. He had a very rugged but distinguished look about him. I would say that he is probably in his mid fifty's. However, who is to judge one's age anyway. He was a two-starred General. His hair looked somewhat gray. His weight is somewhere around 190 pounds. He has brown eyes and wears glasses. He is a well - built muscular man for his age. He must have been rock solid in his younger years. We had about twenty - one trucks left in the fleet. We had enough men for a small war. They had over two hundred thousand rounds of ammunition. About one third of the trucks were loaded with all types of sophisticated equipment.

We have walked in about one mile and had to stop so that the bulldozers could catch up with us. It takes time for them to clear the trees and shrubs out of the way. Then the bulldozers had to level the ground, just enough for the trucks to drive on. We could hear them off in the distance. Therefore, we knew that we were not to far away. We waited until we could see them coming before we took off again. I do not think that we had much farther to go before we ran into the mist.

"How much farther before we run into that mist that you saw?" "Not much farther general." "I believe that it's just over the top of the next hill." "All right then." "Since we are losing daylight, we will camp here for the night." "I don't want anyone to get lost in that mist." "Yes sir, General Hawser." Captain Miller had everyone shut down the equipment as soon as they got close enough to the rest of the group. Then he had them set up camp for the night. The Generals tent was set up in the middle of the rest. This way he was protected. Our tents were set up next to his. They set our tents up this way, not only for our protection, but so we do not have to far to go when we get done going over the game plan with the General. The Captain posted about ten men around the camp on four hour shifts. He wanted to make sure that no one fell asleep at their posts. Some of the trees that were dozed over were cut up for firewood. They had over twenty campfires going around the camp. Everyone was getting settled down for the night. Tomorrow was going to be a long day according to the General. He wanted to make sure that we got enough sleep for tomorrow. Many of the men were very restless. They did not know what would lie ahead of them. Some of them were writing letters to their loved ones back home. I heard that whenever soldiers would come across something that they knew nothing about, they would write home. Some of them wanted to be prepared in case they wouldn't make it back alive.

A few of them complained about having to eat surplus rations. While others complained about having to go into the field without knowing if they were ever coming back. They just wanted their families to know that they loved and missed them very much. Some of them even talked about what they were going to do when they get out of the service.

It is about 6 am and everyone is being woke up. They were told that they were going to break up camp in one and a half hours. Everything must be packed up and ready to go by that time. This included eating their breakfast. The General had called another meeting to make sure that we stuck to our game plan. Doctor Kline wanted to take survey samples from around the surrounding area before we do anything else. He wanted samples just before they enter the mist. Once everyone enters the mist, taking samples from there would be useless. The area would be contaminated from the foot prints. Then after they enter the mist and from around the whole area surrounding the entrance of the pit. He then said that he wanted to send some people down into the pit to see what lies down there besides the mist and slime. He also wants to know when the temperature changes and what levels it changes at. Then he wants to know if the mist stops before they reach the bottom. I said that I want to be one of the people who goes down into the pit, since I was the one who had discovered it.

The General reluctantly agreed to let me go down. But I had some help in that department. Dr. Kline thought it would be a good idea for me to go. He expressed the value of my knowledge and experience in this field. Besides that, I had given them all of my notes and samples from this area. Dr. Kline then said that they would be recording all samples and notes about the area. Then the chosen party will ascend down into the pit after it has been verified safe enough to do so. Our meeting had lasted for about forty-five minutes, That gave us plenty of time to sit down and eat our breakfast.

The time is now 7:30 am and everyone is ready to go. Since I am the one who knows where this is, I will be leading the way. They gave me two body guards to protect me from any danger. Though I didn't think that there will be any. After all, I never did run across any danger on my way through here the first time. Along with them, I have Dr. Kline at my side taking his samples. The four of us are the pack leaders. Behind us was the bulldozers and the rest of the fleet of trucks. We traveled rather slowly so they could keep up with us. It took us twenty-five minutes to get over the top of the hill to the edge of the mist where we waited for the others. We didn't have long to wait. In the mean time, Dr. Kline made good use of his time taking samples and writing down his notes.

First, he took samples from the outside of the mist. Then he walked about ten feet into the mist and took some more samples. He then returned back, to the rest of us. After he had returned, he sat down and wrote about what he saw and experienced. He also noticed a slight temperature change on this side of the mist and another change on the inside of the mist. Just outside of the mist, you could not hear any animal sounds at all. It is almost like they were avoiding this area altogether. Dr. Kline also noticed that the trees were also hard to see. So we got out a rope and tied it up to a tree. This is so the dozers don't get lost. At least the dozers guides will be able to see the rope. I told John that we were not very far away and that we should be extremely careful. Because if we were not, we could fall down into the pit and die. We took the next two hundred yards very slowly. Visual contact with the trees was no longer possible unless we were right next to them.

"I want to stop right here until the others get caught up." "We have gone far enough for the time being." "For we are almost on top of the pit." "So don't anyone stray off." "Yes sir Eric." "We'll make sure that the Doctor doesn't go to far." John continued taking his samples and writing down his notes. I really don't know what he is writing down, but I am sure that it is very important. It did not take to long for the dozers to catch up with us again. I had them wait where they were until I made my estimates of the area. I took three guards and several powerful lanterns to mark the way. I placed them all around the pit. They were only about twenty feet away from the edge of the pit. Then I went back to get the rest of the group marking the trail with lanterns as we went back. John was impatiently waiting. For him, this was a great find. The dozers carefully took down the trees and shrubs surrounding the area in which we were going to be working.

Meanwhile, John was working at the edge of the pit taking more samples. He kept taking samples from all around the pit. Including taking small pieces from the log that rested next to the pit. John was now getting excited like a little kid playing with a new toy. I never knew that scientists ever acted like that. But it was fun to sit back and watch him in action. Dale was busy gathering up all of the samples they took and put them into a steel chest that was made special for the samples. The chest was lined with layers of foam to protect the samples.

It took another five hours for them to clear the land away for all of our equipment, tents, and supplies. By the time all of the tents were set up, it was nearly seven pm. We had spent the whole day taking out a one mile path. I know that everyone is totally beat. They should rest pretty good tonight. The General called another meeting once all of the tents were up. This time he wanted to know some of the results of the samples that were taken. The conclusion was undecided. But they, did say that there were many differences between all of the areas where the samples were taken from. He wanted to know what the differences were.

John told him that each of the samples he took had different colors and textures. He could not believe that there were so many differences. He told the General that whatever this substance was, it seems to control life in every living thing differently. "Without my equipment, I won't know for sure what this is." "I'm going to have my associate Dale and your men work on this while I'm looking into the source of this phenomena." "All right John, but I don't want any wasted time spent on this." "I want every minute of every day accounted for." "After all, I have someone to answer to also." "Yes General, I understand all of that." "They will be making notations on every little detail." "Plus they will be talking with home base to see what conclusions that they have come up with." "They are to keep in close contact every single day or even several times a day if they have any breakthroughs." "That is all there is for now." "Is that god enough General?" "Yes, that will have to be good enough." "I'm calling an end to this meeting until tomorrow morning at seven am, after breakfast." "I hope that you all get some sleep tonight."

Everyone had left for his or her own tents. Along the way to our tent, John had noticed how wet the tents were starting to get on the outside. He recorded that at night, the area seemed to get wet three times faster than it did during the day. A few hours had passed by. Everyone was sound asleep. There was a rustling noise coming through the camp. It woke up everyone that it went by. As soon as they had poked their heads out of their tents, the noise had completely disappeared into the mist. Nobody even got a chance to catch a glimpse of what it was. They quickly grabbed their guns and lanterns. They started to search the entire area around the camp to see if there was anything missing or damaged. One man found a trail that had been left behind, by whatever it was that had come through the camp. He called out for the others to come so they could follow the trail to see where it may lead.

"Don't touch anything on the trail." "I want to see for myself what it is." said the Doctor. He took samples off of the trail as he went along. It had lead him right to the very edge of the pit and disappeared without a trace. He took a few more samples and gave them to Dale. Dale immediately packed them up and had them sent to the lab by a special courier. Then Dale walked back over to where John was. "I want to know what that is tonight Dale." "I need to know if that is blood or what." "Okay John, if you say so." "You can always get some sleep in the morning Dale." "I guess that you are right John." "We do need to find out what that really is." Dale went to stop the courier before he got a chance to leave with the samples. He then took the samples back to his tent and started working on them. It took him four hours to finish all of the tests. He had worked very hard on the tests to finish them before it got light out. He then called John over to him.

"Well there are traces of animal blood and other substances mixed together." "What kind of animal blood, I can't tell you." "But I can say that the substance we are investigating, is devouring the blood as we speak." "Okay Dale, you can go get some sleep now." "You have done well." "There's not to many hours left." "You can sleep in late if you like." "I'll take over from here." "Thanks John." "I am really beat." "I'll see you some time in the morning John." "Okay Dale." "You had better get some rest while you can." Everyone had settled back down for the rest of the night. During that time, there were no more noises throughout the remainder of the night.

It was about 8:30 am when they all woke up. There was no sunshine, but there was some light. It was almost like a cloudy day, dark and dismal. Breakfast was being served in the mess tent. They were having ham, bacon, sausage, eggs, pancakes, toast and coffee. There was even orange juice for those who wanted it. The men who had finished their breakfast were hard at work. They were setting up all kinds of equipment. One piece was a gas powered generator. So that we could have electricity to work with. I also saw them putting up some high powered work lights around the entire camp. Some men were in the process of setting up the crane over the entrance of the pit. They also had a fence put up around the pit to keep us from falling in. One man was filling up the tank on the generator from the fully loaded tanker. They had enough fuel to last about three months.

I walked over to John's tent. He was putting on a protective suit. He looked over at me. "Put on the suit." "It's time for us to go down into the pit." "Is there anyone else going down there with us?" "Yes there is Eric." "There are eight more men putting their suits on as we speak." "They will be carrying some of the equipment and their weapons." The suits were made of some thick plastic material, but light weight. The only consisted of one piece with two different sets of zippers on the side. One was about six inches from the other one. Once they were zipped up, nothing would be able to penetrate the suit. They were completely water tight. Then we put on our air tanks. We were bringing these along just to be on the safe side. John did not know whether or not, the air was poisonous to us. We checked each other over to make sure that we put everything on correctly.

"What about this Geiger Counter?" "Do you think that we will need it?" "Yes we do." "While your at it, grab the Atmospheric Tester." "I want to check for radioactivity and poisonous gases while we are down there." "Do you think that there really is any radioactivity or poisonous gases down there John?" "Eric, you never know until you get down there." "Even though its safe up here, it could be very deadly down there." "You never know what to expect until you are actually in that situation." All other preparations have been made. We are now ready to go down into the pit. When we got over to the pit, the others were waiting for us. They were already standing in a large basket fully equipped with work lights shinning in all directions. This would definitely make it easier for us to see. Everyone was equipped with a radio to maintain contact with the surface.

This was also so that we could keep in touch with each other as well. In case we were to get separated from one another. They had attached a radio to the basket for our ease. The basket itself could only handle ten people at the most. A much larger basket was being constructed for us. This reminded John of a poem that he has written.

> As we enter the forbidden abyss,
> The darkness will over whelm you,
> A black cloud engulfs you without a hiss,
> Sinking deeper and deeper and through
> Leaving no feelings ever untouched,
> Clinging to one's body like a clamp,
> Causing you to shudder ever so much,
> Turning the tables as we camp.
> Forcing you to look into the dark black void,
> Imagining things that are rift really there,
> Sounds ring from a druid,
> Threatening to bring you to bear.
> Seeing thoughts you need to see,
> While trying to laugh it off,
> Leaning toward ones own tree,
> Dancing all over ones own scoff.

After everyone was aboard the basket, it was picked up and slowly lowered down into the pit. We went down five hundred feet. John told them to stop for a few minutes. "Take a look at the walls." "Do you see anything different about the walls?" "The walls are very smooth and has a shine to them." "They shine as though they had been polished." "You can almost see yourself in them." "The walls also seem to run in a perfect circle." "Precisely Eric." "It seems like you have done your homework real well." "This pit was not made by a natural cause." "It leans more to a manmade one." "But I myself have never seen one made so perfectly." "So what could have made this the way that it is now?" "Eric, do you have any ideas about this?" "After all, you are the leading expert in this field." "No John, I don't have a single clue." "I myself have never seen anything like it before."

John took samples of the surface of the wall. Hoping that by doing this, it would give him some clues to how this wall was made. Then he had them lower the basket again. We went down another five hundred feet and stopped. He took some more samples nom the wall. Then he took the readings nom the Geiger Counter and the Atmospheric Tester. The readings from both checked out to be safe at this level. That seemed to have puzzled him a bit. When he was done, he had them lower us the rest of the way down-until we hit the bottom of the pit. The basket sank about two inches into the slime. He again took the readings nom the Geiger Counter and the Atmospheric Tester. They both still read well into the safe margin. He just could not understand why this was happening. But he did accept it for the time being.

John radioed up to the surface and asked if it were safe to walk on the slime. The answer came back five minutes later. It was safe enough to walk on the slime with our suits on.

CHAPTER Two

W e looked around and saw four entrances to underground tunnels. This had struck John in a very peculiar way. He did not know what to think of this. He immediately called up for more men. They asked him why he wanted more men. He told them that there were some tunnels down here and he wanted to start searching them. They asked how many men he would like to have. He told them that he wanted sixty more men. They told him that it would be at least one hour before they could come down. They had to change the baskets and get the men suited up. John told them that he wanted them fully equipped. and for them not to forget the lanterns this time. John's group stepped into the tunnel to keep from being dripped on as they raised the basket back up to the surface. We did not want to take any chances down here. Besides we had no idea of what could be waiting for us up ahead. John told them to be careful of the basket. Because there was lots of slime dripping off of it. After the basket had been raised up, John had his men start searching the area for the remains of a dead animal. What they had found was a small dead weasel. All that remained were just a few un-dissolved bones. Whatever else there was, may have been completely destroyed.

The hour had gone by very quickly and they called us back. They said that the men were on their way down. That we would be able to see them coming at any time. No sooner had they said that, we were able to see them coming down. It only took them five more minutes for the basket to hit the bottom. This basket was definitely much larger. It almost took up the entire area. They had also sent down more men than what he had asked for. They had sent him forty men over what he originally had asked for. That had made a total of one hundred men that they had sent down. At least they were fully equipped. Among the men that were sent, was his colleague Dale McCoy and Captain Miller. They all gathered around to discuss who would go where. There were four tunnels and one hundred and ten men to go in. They each took twenty-seven men apiece. They left two behind to stand guard at the basket. They all left at the same time.

Some of the things that they had talked about was to keep our heads in the right places and to think about safety at all times. Another one was that if there were any sign of danger, for us to call in to the other groups. Then John told us what to look out for and keep him informed of what we were doing at all times. Then the last thing that he wanted from us, was for us to keep taking samples every so many yards. We all had gone down our own tunnels to explore. The tunnel that my group had entered was similar to the pit. The tunnel had a symmetrical shape to it. The height of the tunnel was at about twelve feet. It looks smooth in some areas and rough in others.

We have walked in about seventy-five feet. The mist is still thick and its quite hard to see. We kept on walking, being on the alert for anything to happen. We were walking very slowly for now. We walked about another twenty-five yards into the tunnel. Then suddenly, we came right out of the mist. I had my men keep on coming until they all were out of the mist altogether. Then I started to look around a bit to see if I could see why the mist had stopped flowing this way. I looked everywhere, but I could not find anything. Then one of my men had spotted something on top of the ceiling of the tunnel. Right at the edge of the mist was a spout about ten inches around. It was facing towards the pit. Maybe that is why the mist did not come this way. The strangest thing is that none of us can even feel a draft. So why doesn't the mist flow this way as well? I ordered one of my men to start taking photos of the area and the rest of the journey. I then reported my findings to John. He said that his group was still in the mist. He then wanted to know if we were still walking in the slime. I told him that we were and that I couldn't see no end to it. Dale And Captain Miller both reported the mist and the slime.

We collected all of our samples. Including a sample of the mist and put them in our packs. After that, I assigned two of my men to collect all of the samples from here on in. We then pushed farther into the tunnel, picking up our pace as we went along. We have been walking for about two hours and everything still remained the same. I asked the men how they were doing. They said that they were doing fine. So I decided to keep on going. The Geiger Counter was still reading well within the normal perimeters. The slime is still clear and still about two inches deep. None of us had any idea of what the slime is or even where it was coming from. I radioed in to the main base to find out what they came up with. They said that the results of the tests were still inconclusive. They said that they will keep testing the slime for everything that they can think of. I told them to let me know as soon as they came up with something. Then I called the General and asked him to have some of his men set up two satellite dishes, one at the top of the pit and one at the bottom of the pit. This was to make sure that we did not lose contact with one another. He said that he would make sure that they get it done. I heard him assign three of his men to do the job. I told the General that I would check back in with him in about three hours unless we find something. He said no, that would not work at all. He wants us to check in every hour on the hour. I told him that I would. The other three groups said that they would too. I told the radio man to keep checking in with the General as he instructed. So far no one in any of the groups have run across anything new to report. We continued on.

We have been walking for about forty-five minutes and we were forced to stop dead in our tracks. The slime had come to an end. Five feet in front of us was a four inch high step holding back the slime. Then twenty-five feet from there were three more tunnels branching off from this one. We walked over to the entrance of the tunnels and stopped there so I could call in my findings. I reported to the General and told him that three more tunnels exist. He said that he would send down more troops. He told me to leave some of my men behind to guard the entrance. Then they can tell the others which way to go. I told him that I would do that. I chose five men who would stay behind. I told the General that the troops should take the tunnel on the far left. Then I am taking the tunnel on the right again. He said that the troops will be there in about three hours. I took the rest of the men with me, leaving only the five guards behind. As we disappeared from their view, I could see a light begin to burn. They apparently lit up a lantern so that they do not have to stay in the dark. For being down here with no light can make a man go crazy very easily. The walls would seem like they are crashing down upon you in the black of the night. For being down here in the dark is absolutely nothing to see. You would not even be able to see your own hand in front of your nose. It is like being born blind. I am glad that they were smart enough to light their lanterns.

We have been walking for about fifty-three minutes this time. We came upon a huge gigantic entrance. We slowed down again. We then proceeded with extreme caution. The entrance was getting closer and closer. Until we suddenly came through the entrance and discovered that we came into a huge cavern. I held up my hand for my men to stop immediately. I quickly got on the radio to the General to inform him that we have stumbled onto a very large cavern. The General told me to hold up here until the new troops arrive. I said that would be fine because my men needed to get some rest anyway. He said that they were only two hours behind me now. I asked the General how many men he had sent me. He told me that he had sent down fifty men. He said that Sergeant Ted Banks was leading them in. I told the general that I would call in again when the others get here. He said that would be fine. Then I spoke to Ted and told him to leave two more men at the second tunnel with the other five. He told me that he would do that.

I started looking around and I could no longer see the top of the ceiling. I had no idea how deep this cavern was. "One of you men take a look around and see what you can find." "But don't go to far." "I don't want anyone getting lost in here." "Yes sir," they replied. They discussed between themselves which one would go. He got up and disappeared into the dark. The rest of us continued to sit on the very hard ground while we waited for the troops to catch up with us. The smell of the cavern was starting to get to me. It has been a long time since I was in one like this. The strong smell of musk was all around us. Not only was the smell getting to me, but the sense of being encased in rock was beginning to over whelm me too. I knew that I had to keep my head clear and my wits about me for the sake of my men. For I was their only leader who knows what to do down here in the pits of everlasting darkness.

I called John and asked him if he has found anything new. "We are still walking through the mist and can't see a thing as of yet." "How far do you think that you may have gone John?" "Well Eric, I would estimate that we have gone about seven miles." "We have stopped from time to time to take our samples." "I really don't expect to find anything here." "But you can never tell what will come up." "Yes, I already found that out." "Did you hear my reports to the General?" "Yes I did." "That was good thinking on your part." "It sure was a good idea for you to come along." "Your expertise in this field will come in very handy." "Thank you John." "I am certainly glad that someone thinks so."

Dale reported that he was still in the mist. He said that he kept taking samples to be sure that they were not changing. He said that he would check back in an hour. Captain Miller said that his tunnel seemed to be getting a little larger. But he also was still walking in the mist. He then said that his samples were beginning to change a bit. He said that the slime had also gotten one inch deeper. "Some of the rock surfaces are turning different colors." "Some are yellow, blue, orange, red, and green." "All of them are in separate areas from one another." "None of them are close enough together to make any kind of judgment on." "I took samples of each and every one, hoping that it will make a difference in the long run." Then Sergeant Banks came back on. He told me that he left two men at the fork and that he should catch up to me in about half an hour.

"Great, then we can get going again." My other man had just come back. "What did you find?" "Sir:" "Don't call me sir." "Call me by my name which is Eric." "I found nothing at all." "But this cavern goes on for about one and a half miles to the right." "It doesn't stay as large as it does here." "It is about five times smaller than this one." "As far as the other two directions, I haven't got the slightest clue how far it goes." One of my men heard some sort of noise coming from the background and yelled out. "Who goes there?" "Sergeant Banks at your command sir." "Good, do your men need to rest yet?" "No sir." "My men are eager to go on." "All right then, lets get going." "We have much work to finish up."

We started out again. But now I have eighty-seven men in my command. I had my men spread out so we could cover more ground. We walked and walked and walked. I thought that we would never come to the end of this cavern. But we finally did. Unfortunately, we have not found anything else to report to General Hawser. I told him that we were going back to one of the other tunnels. He told me to keep in touch. I told him that since we have not found anything new, I felt that it was safe enough for us not to call in for a couple of hours. He said okay, but I am not to make a habit of it. I said fine. It took one hour forty-five minutes to get back to the fork. Then we went down the middle tunnel. My other men were still there, safe and sound. In no time at all, we went in pretty far. We covered one and one half miles in twenty-three minutes. It was time for my next report. I halted my men so I could take some samples before I called in. I noticed that the walls were sweating. Down on the ground, the substance looked like a milky color. I scraped some up and put it into a test tube. The walls also showed a change. They were somehow crystallizing. Whatever this stuff was, it was causing several different effects. My samples box was completely full. I had completely run out of bottles. So I traded boxes with one of my men. Then I sent him back to the camp for another one. I informed the General that I had sent a man back to him for fresh supplies. I also told the General about the changes that I have found in this area. He told me to be careful until he can get the samples tested to see if it was safe or not.

I asked John if he heard my report to the General. He said that he did. He asked me if I had noticed any other changes in here. I looked around a bit more. I still could not see anything else that was different. I told him no, there was not. He said that I might begin to see other changes farther down the line. He informed me that this substance could be a form of an Amino Acid. It was completely harmless, but he had to be sure of it. He asked me to stay where I was until the results came back from the main base. I told him that I would wait until further notice. I asked him how far in he was. He told me that he had covered about seven miles. Nor has he found anything new. I thought that this was really strange, since I was running into all sorts of changes. I told him that I was about three miles in, on count of back tracking.

To help pass the time by, I called up Dale and Captain Miller. I asked them what was happening. Dale said that he was puzzled by this. He said that the secretion had to be coming from somewhere and I should be watching for more changes in the area. He said that it could be very close. I told him that we would keep our eyes open. I asked him how far in he has traveled. He said that he was in about eight miles if his calculations were correct. He also said that the mist was very thin. So he could see much better than he was able to before. He said that he had walked out of the slime about four miles back. He also sent back one of his men for fresh supplies. I told my men that they better eat while they have the chance. But not to leave any trash lying around. I want to leave these tunnels in the same condition that they were found in. Then I asked Captain Miller what he had found. He said that the slime was getting a little deeper. But the mist was completely gone. He said that the walls were still very smooth and shiny. They were also still multi-colored. He also said that the walls were reflecting light back at them. Making it much easier for them to see. I said that the crystals have a tendency to do that. "At least that is what I have discovered in other caverns that I have been in." He also said that it felt like they were going downhill. But he couldn't be sure. He said everything looks the same but yet different. I told him that it was just an illusion and that he probably was going downhill.

Dale asked Captain Miller how deep the slime was. Captain Miller got out his ruler and measured it. He told Dale that it was about four inches deep. Dale said that he wants him to measure it every fifteen feet. So he can get an idea of what is happening in that tunnel. Captain Miller said that he would. I checked to see what time it was. I could not believe that it was already 5 pm.

Meanwhile back on top of the surface, the General was making plans of his own. "Soldier, get me the Pentagon." "I want to talk to the Chief of Staff" "Yes sir General Hawser." "The Chief is on the line sir." The soldier handed him the phone. "Chief, General Hawser here." "I have a good feeling that 1 am going to need more men and equipment." "I want permission to take soldiers from anywhere in the country and bring them here." "No sir, it is not like that at all." "I just don't want to be surprised." "I want to be ready for anything." "Please let me explain sir." "Those men down there are constantly running into new tunnels." "As far as I know, those tunnels could run for hundreds of miles." "I don't have the slightest clue as to how many men that I will need." "I might only need five hundred or five million." "I just don't know." "How can you judge the unknown?" "Thank you sir." "You have a pleasant day to." "Click," the General hung up the phone.

"That's great." "I feel like celebrating." "The Chief of Staff just gave me complete authorization to call in as many troops as 1 may need." "Soldier, I want you to call three of the closet bases and have them send me five thousand men and equipment from each one." "Yes sir General." Then the general had his men clear out tour hundred square yards of land for the new troops that would be coming in. That would make a total of six hundred square yards of land that has been cleared. He was afraid that if he had cleared anymore than that, the Chief of Staff would take and bust him back down to a private. He wasn't going to let that happen. After all, this was a public forest and a National Wildlife Refuge. He then told them to keep all of the small branches to use as firewood. The rest of it will be stacked up and hauled off at a later date. Then I came up with a brainstorm of an idea. I decided to call the general and ask him what he thought of it. "General Hawser, this is Eric." "I came up with a plan to get rid of all of this mist down here." "How about if we get some six inch pipe and run it from the hole along the ceiling to the outside." "Then we would have a vent and the air would start to clear up." "Maybe then we will be able to see a lot easier."

General Hawser said that would be a great idea and he would call for a few truck loads of pipe. The he would have his engineers start working on it. He said that it would probably take about twelve hours for all of it to get here.

Then Captain Johnson called in with some good news. He said that they found out that salt water mixes with the slime. Then when its heated, it turns into a rubbery substance that hardens after it cools. Then you can use it for a road to drive on. "That is definitely good news." "Well done men." "Keep up the good work and let me know when you come up with some more good news." "We will try Dr. Kline." "We are also sending you the necessary equipment to get this job done." "Three trucks full of salt water and about ten flame throwers." "That should get the job done." "Captain Johnson, you are a good man." "You men there at the lab are a vital key to our research." "Thank you from all of us Dr. Kline." The men that had been sent to the surface are finally on their way back to their groups. With fresh supplies for taking their samples. All of the groups are getting restless and want to continue on. But they can't until their supplies gets back to them. I got a report that my man is almost here. I am glad to have heard that. For I am tired of waiting around. I only had to wait for half an hour more than before, which was not to long. My supplies are finally here at last.

The time is 8:30 pm and we have much territory to cover. We will probably end up staying here all night. We started out again and only walked about fifty yards when we came to a new surprise. Our tunnel is starting to go uphill. Who knows where this will lead. I decided to hold off on my report until I have more proof on what we are experiencing. The walls are no longer smooth. But are instead bumpy and jagged. The color is jet black, almost like coal. Then another startling surprise. The passage is getting narrower. It is no longer ten feet wide. We have gone another two miles into the tunnel and its still only six feet wide.

The time is now 9:30 pm. We still have not come to the end of the tunnel. But hopefully we will find out what is at the end of this one. Me and my men have definitely had a very long day. Maybe we will find a spot to camp for the night. The passage is still only six feet wide and we were still going uphill. I do not know how far we have gone, but I am sure that we will find out. The other groups have already called in. The general is hollering for me to answer. I really do not want to, but maybe I had better. Just so he does not send a rescue party in after us. I told the general that we have gone a few more miles up into the passage. I also had told him all of my findings and that we will keep going until we find a place to camp for the night. He told me not to be late again or else. I told him that I held off for those reasons. He could have been a bit more patient with me. But you know how these big shots are, always in a hurry. Seems like they can never wait for anything. Two of the other groups have stopped for the night. Their men were to tired to keep on going. The third group is still pushing on trying to find a place where they can stop for the night. We have gone another mile and a half. We finally came out into another huge cavern. I had my men spread out fifty feet to the right and thirty feet to the left. On the left there was a wall and on the right there was a large drop off. Two of my men shined their lights down towards the bottom. They told me that they could see the bottom. It was about two hundred feet down. Then they shined their lights straight out and could not see anything at all. The beams just disappeared into the dark. This could be an upper chamber, that is part of the bottom one. I told my men to head over to the wall and make camp for the night. That will give everyone a chance to rest before we start out again in the morning. It was 10:20 pm and I called the general to let him know that we were staying at this point for the night. He told me that this was a perfect place for us. I then told him that there won't be any more contact from us until 6:00 am. That is when we will start out again. He said that he will be sending in more troops in the morning to dry up all of the slime. Then they will find the mist holes and vent them to the outside area.

I had a hard time trying to sleep. The night air of the caverns comes crashing down on you like a ton of bricks. The temperature often has a tendency to let you know that it is only 60 degrees. But no matter what, life must go on. So you stay warm as much as possible. Slowly I began to drift off into a deep sleep. While Eric and the others slept, four guards remained on duty. They quietly walked up and down the area to make sure that all of the others were safe and kept from harm. If anything were to happen, they would alert the others immediately. The air in the cavern made it easy for the men to sleep very soundly. When it was time for the change of the guard, they went and woke up the next four that were chosen for duty. The entire night went on that way until 6:00 am. Then the guards woke up the others. Eric immediately called up the general to explain that they were all right. Then they would contact him again in two hours. This time the general agreed to it. Eric felt relieved. He thought for sure that he would be in hot water up to his neck. But he was wrong. Eric told his men to eat their breakfast so they could go on through the tunnels.

It was 6:30 am and they were ready to go on. Before they were going to leave, Eric decided to take one of the lanterns and let it dangle from the upper ledge. If the two were the same, the next group would know. That would also save them some time since they had the know how to climb up to the top without any trouble at all. The general had plans of his own. If things went well enough, he would try to move more troops in. But one thing at a time had to happen first. He did not want to put the cart before the horse or he would fall. Eric and his men had been walking for about one hour. But he had not come to the end of the cavern yet. It seemed to have branched off the other one. It was getting close to the time when Eric was supposed to check in with the general. So he decided to go ahead and check in a bit early.

The time was 7:45 am. He checked in with the general. The general told him that they had already begun to harden up the slime. Eric told him that he had dangled a lantern from the upper cavern. If they can find it from the lower one, that would mean that he was right. He then told the general that he has not come to the end of the cavern yet. But he is looking all around and there is nothing else to report. The general told Eric to report back in, in two more hours. The Captain's group was going deeper into the tunnel. They were still going downhill. Captain Miller kept checking the depth of the slime like he was suppose to. At this point, the slime was about six inches deep and it seemed to be getting deeper by the hour. He has traveled about fifteen miles in and he can find no end to the tunnel. He had finished making his report to the general. The slime was very thick. It made their walking much harder, because it was so deep. They never knew that walking could be so difficult. The multi-colored walls were beginning to change a bit. They looked like they were forming into different types of patterns. The Captain took out his notebook and jotted down the new details. He was careful not to leave anything out. For it might be important at a later time. Dr. Kline had been in the mist since yesterday. Apparently his group spent the night in the mist. They had only covered eight miles. It was much to hard for them to go any faster. Compared to the rest of the groups, they were moving along like snails. But no one can criticize them. For they had no control over the entire matter. If he had his way, he would have walked about twenty miles already. But it was completely out of his control. All of his reports were basically the same. He had no new discoveries or changes to be made. As for the existence of the tunnels, no one had any clue as to how they were formed or even made. This was still a mystery to them all.

It is now 10:30 am and many things were beginning to happen. The general had completed the first stage of the main pit. All of the slime had been hardened up. He had begun to lower more equipment down into the bottom of the pit. Only four jeeps could fit down there at a time. So he had to wait for his men on the cleanup crew to finish on one of the tunnels. This was a fairly slow process and he did not want to push his luck with it. At least he was able to get three crews into the tunnels to harden up the slime. With three crews going at once, the job will move along much faster. After all, he wanted to be sure that all of his men were safe.

After the jeeps were lowered down to the bottom, there was no room for anything else to be brought down. The cleanup crews started on the tunnels very quickly, in order to get the equipment down there. I completed another three miles in this cavern and still have not found the end of it. I thought that this area would make a great underground base while the rest of us were exploring these tunnels. I will be glad when I come to the end of this cavern. I really want to see what lies ahead in the last tunnel. This cavern seems to be so large, that you could put an entire city in it. I am sure that the army will make good use of it. How far does this thing go anyway? I kept thinking that on every step that I took. I heard Dr. Kline's report come through for the fourth time today. It must be 12:30 pm. It sure is. I had my men stop and take a break for half an hour. They looked like they needed it. I know that I did. This report was a long one. He must have found something. He said that he walked another five miles in the mist and suddenly came out of it all at once. On the other side of the mist, he came directly out into a huge gigantic cavern. he said that it seemed to go all of the way to the surface. But yet he couldn't feel any breeze or wind at all. It was completely calm. The reason for this statement was that this cavern was lit up by the surface. Inside this cavern, he was able to see many types of vegetation. Including several types of trees. At least that this is what they looked like.

He could see Ferns., Grass, Ivy's, and shrubs among the trees. Some of the trees had different types of moss growing on them. He could not believe what he was seeing. "How did these get all the way down here?"

Everyone who had heard this report was given a shock treatment. They could not answer him at all. John said that he would be in there for quite some time taking all kinds of samples. Then he was going to try to analyze the reason for this new discovery. He even said that some vines were even growing on the wall where he was standing. He told the general that he was going to be busy for quite a while and for no one to disturb him. He told the general that when he comes up with some clues, that he will give them a call. The general said that he will allow him five hours and then he must call in. John said that would work out just fine. Then John went off the air. That was the strangest thing that I have ever heard of in my entire life. I have absolutely no idea of how this could be possible. In my mind, this was totally impossible. This just could not be. But yet, John said that it is there. How did it get there? That was such a shock to me, that I could hardly move for about ten minutes. My men had been laughing all this time. Thinking that Dr. John Kline was on some kind of drug. I told them to shut up and listen to what I have to say about underground caverns. I told them that I myself, had seen many strange things before. But this one was the strangest one that I have ever heard. If I had not of set them straight, they would not have believed what they had heard John say.

Dale said that he still has not found anything new to report. That he would continue on until it was time for his next report. Captain Miller on the other hand did find something new. He had come to a cavern himself. It was somewhat dim lit. The part where the slime was, started to continue downhill and he came to a dry place where he and his men could walk without getting any slime on them at all. About fifty feet in front of him, he could see a bridge made of stone going over the slime. The bridge was over forty-two feet long. There was enough room on the bridge for only one jeep to cross over at a time. It had spike like things made of stone sticking up from the side of the bridge. Creating something like a wall to prevent a jeep from going over the side. On the outside edge of the bridge, you can see some carvings shaped like symbols. But they were unable to make them out. It apparently was a new type of language that we have never seen before. On the other side was a plateau where they could walk. He said that they were going to stay right there until more help could arrive. He also said, from what he could see is that the slime had been formed into what seemed to be a river and disappeared out of his line of sight. He said that without any more help, that he would be taking a big chance on losing his men. He simply did not want that to happen. The general told him that it would be several hours or even the next day before anyone could get to him. He said that they will still wait. That it would not be a problem at all. Wow, I said to myself. That was a total of three new discoveries. All in one day too. What else could be waiting for us to discover? Is there still more to come? Or is this the end of it all? No matter what happens, I will continue to find out more. Now my men really did believe what they had heard. They knew their Captain real well and they themselves knew that he would never imagine to see something that wasn't there. They no longer had any doubts about Dr.

Kline and what he had found. Dale was beginning to get disappointed. Because he was the only one who really has not made a discovery out of the ordinary. But I told him to be patient. If anything is there, that he will be the first to find it. The General came back on the air and told us all that he was sending us more troops as soon as they get there. He also said that he was going to have his men working around the clock to complete all of the repairs. For he wants to move all of the operations down here. He himself wants to see all of these new and grand wonders. This exploration has now become a complete military operation. That no one is to leak any of this information out to the public. He said that when the time comes, he will allow it to be heard by the rest of the world. I told General Hawser that since this was my discovery, that I, personally wanted all of the credit. He told me that there are three others that I must share the credit with. Since they made their own discoveries down here. I told him no. That is was I who originally made the discovery and I sought the help of others. The General then said that it would go down like this. If, I did not give them some of the credit, that he personally, would discredit me from all of the discoveries and he would give the credit to the other three. He said that I would have the main or most of the credit. I told him that sounded better, because I really do not have any choice in the matter. I told him that he made his point and I will obey his decision. The General told me that when he is done here, that the four of us will be filthy rich and famous. Then we will never have to worry about money ever again. Then the General informed me that I now work for the army as a civilian and that I have a top security clearance. This way I can get onto any base in the country to see what is going on. I told him thanks. That was great. I always wanted to know what really went on behind closed doors. He told me that now I will get the chance to see what they do and work on. But that I am not to ever reveal anything that I may happen to see or hear. I said that I will agree to that. "Anything you say General Hawser."

By this time, I got the notion to look at my watch. It was nearly 1:30 pm. This was the busiest that the air waves has been since we started out yesterday. By now, I was feeling very proud of myself. I managed to become a very important person without even trying. How lucky could I get. My men told me to snap out of it. They said that I was starting to daydream. And for me to come back out of the clouds. Then they called me a big shot. I informed them that I am not a big shot. I am just a man with more responsibility. They said yes, but that I am now one of their bosses. That they must take all orders that I give them, no matter what it is. I told them that I would never put them in any danger. That I will put myself in danger first. They told me that they could not let that happen. For it was their job to protect me. After all, I was more valuable to the government now. I said point taken, but for them not to worry. I will do my best to keep us all out of harms way. They told me that they were proud to have me as their leader.

We have covered another fives miles in this cavern and still there was no end to it. Where or when is this going to end or stop? The answer will eventually come up. Down here, nature has no rules to go by. Every step we take may put our lives in danger. But, it is our job to take those chances. We must make the best of it. Captain Miller made his next report. He said it was 3:00 pm and his group is doing fine. They are patiently waiting for them to be reached. The General told him that the slime had been taken care of in two of the tunnels. They are trying to finish the other two. He then said that the crew for sealing up the leaks, had just been sent in. They finally had enough room to send down a few more jeeps. One with a trailer for the conduit, cement, and hangers. He said that it should not be to many more hours before he can send down any more men and equipment. He said that they are working as fast as they can possibly go. Captain Miller said that he'll be waiting for them to show up. Dale called in. He said that he went about another five miles and has nothing to report yet. At least that is how he feels. The General told him to keep going. That there must be something there. He said that he had a strange feeling about it. Dale said that he would like to know what it is. But the General could not put a finger on it. He said that it was just a feeling. The General estimated that Dale has gone in about twenty or thirty miles inside of that particular tunnel. He also said that Dale is in the deepest so far. And that he should be extremely careful. There is no telling what can happen. Dale said that he was being careful and that he will check in about two hours.

The cavern that I was just in, emptied out into a much larger one than I was just in. This one was lit up by the surface. Just like the one that Dr. John Kline is in. I can see several different levels right from where I stand. There must be at least five that I can count straight ahead. But to either side is to far away to tell. I do not know if there are any in here. But I will certainly find out. We walked straight ahead for about half a mile and came to a sudden stop. We were at what seemed to be the edge of the level in which we were standing on. As I looked down, I could count several more levels. There must be at least ten more. Each of them were about two hundred feet apart. The other side looked like it was only a half mile away. But the level on the other side was something else. I could not see where it ended. Not even with my binoculars. This was extraordinarily most unbelievable. Yet again, it is real enough. It has to be. Because it is right in front of me. This one must cover several miles.

I would like to know who built this. As I look just to the right of the levels in front of me, are some more. They seem to be staggered from each other. Then when I looked to the left, I can see the same thing. They also look like they are about two hundred feet apart in that direction too. Who ever thought of this was a genius. I would love to meet this person. I told my men to take a break while I call this in to the general. "Calling General Hawser." "General Hawser, are you there?" "This is Eric calling." "Are you still at home?"

"Quit clowning around Eric." "What do you have for me?" "Well General, your not going to believe this one." "Try me anyway Eric."

"We have just entered a much larger cavern, than what we were just in." "It is lit up from the surface." "Just like the one that Dr. Kline is in." "And there are several different levels." "To many for us to count." "The other difference is that I ca not see the end of the other side, and or, in any other direction." "It also goes way down deep into the ground." "I was able to count five going up from where I stand." "But they are also staggered like building blocks." "I do not see any form of vegetation here as of yet." "We have not had a chance to look around." "I thought that I would give you a call first." "Eric, you did the right thing." "I think you better wait right there until I can get some more troops down there to you." "Yes sir General Hawser." "We will wait right here." "What about the other tunnel?" "That one will have to wait until you finish this one." "But this one could take weeks or even months to completely check out." "I ca not spread you men out that far Eric." "I want you to have enough men to protect you." "Yes sir, I understand." "And we will wait for more men." "Your men will be there in about three hours."

The time is 5:00 pm. The Captain called in again. Asking how much longer that they had to wait. The General said that the crew was about half way into the tunnel. They were getting the slime faster than they thought that they would. Captain Miller said they would stay put. Dr Kline called in with startling results. He said that there was not any soil underneath any of the plant life. But somehow the roots have been altered so that they could grow right through the rock floor. There was also a pool of water that seemed to be spring fed where he was at. He said that he has not had a chance to go any farther than what he did. Every plant is of brilliant green and so much alive. He also said that the cavern was much larger than he had thought. The next step was to check all around the edge of the cavern to see what else he could find. He said that he will check back before it got to dark to see. But they will stay there for the night.

The General told him good luck and to be careful. He then signed off and went about his business. Dale was the only one left. He had just called in. He said that he has gone another six miles and he still could not believe how deep he was going into the tunnel. He and his men have been walking for almost two days and have not found anything new or exciting to report about.

Dale sounded like he was getting very discouraged. But he knew that he must go on, no matter what. He was also beginning to wonder if this particular tunnel had an end or if it would go on forever. He just did not really know. That is all he had to say on the air. The General did say one good thing to him. He told Dale how proud he was of him for not giving up. But so far, Dale had stuck it out. Then the air went silent.

In the mean time, the piping crew was half finished. They had the conduit strung all the way to the main tunnel. Where they had to branch it off and temporarily cap the end of the y pipe until it is needed for the other tunnel. Then they had the crane operator lowered the basket with their supplies, so that they could finish the job.

Each piece was about twenty feet long. They had over one mile to go. They put one section on after another. It took them fifteen minutes to put on each section. After about three hours, they had almost reached the top. They only had about five hundred feet to go before they did reach the top of the pit. This part of the job was very time consuming and they all knew it. They figured that they will have the job completed in about six or eight more hours. They will be able to finish the job in about one-third the time. If most of the men get involved.

Back down in the tunnels, the slime crew had only one mile to go before they reached the Captain. They had called him on the radio to let him know that it would not be much longer. The Captain said that he was glad to hear that. The Captain told them that he would wait at the point where they were supposed to stop. He told them that if they were to go any farther than that, they could possibly sink instead of staying on top of it. After all, the Captain had plenty of time to test the depth of the slime. The crew leader said that he would accept that and be grateful for the help that he can get. He said that it will make his job not only easier, but move more swiftly. It did not seem to take to long for the crew to meet up with the Captain. The Captain showed the crew exactly where to stop. It was just a few feet beyond the point where the jeep could drive up onto the rocky ground. Once on top of the upper area, the jeep would be able to turn around without any trouble. Then the crew quickly finished up the job and headed back to the pit to get more supplies. They only had one more tunnel to finish. When they got back to the pit, there was a new crew waiting to take over. They showed the crew which tunnel to take.

At this time it was already 8 pm. The piping crew was already outside of the pit. Working on the main level, trying to finish the last section of pipe. They had received all the help that they wanted. That right there made their job much easier.

The General had sent down thirty-five hundred soldiers. Standing by waiting for their equipment to come down. As the jeeps came down, they were sent in Eric's direction. Each fully loaded with supplies. Plus the jeeps had an empty wagon for the men to ride in. Each wagon could hold about twenty men. They had brought down eighty jeeps to start with. The men climbed into the vehicles as they came down into the pit and took off towards their destination. They split up going down each of the tunnels. This was the only way the General could supply the groups with the men that they all were asking for. He told them that it would take a few days for all of the men to get there. So they had to be patient and stay where they are.

He planned on sending them each five thousand men to start with. He told them to make camp there until all of the men had shown up. He told them that he would notify them as soon as the last ones are coming down. Then at that time, they can start to break up their camps. He said with the caverns as large as they may be, that they will take all the help that they can get. Then if they wanted to break up into smaller groups, they will be able to do so.

The General was able to send down four hundred men at a time. When he sent them down to wait for the jeeps to follow, they had to wait along the walls of the tunnels so the jeeps were still able to get through. It takes one hour for the men to go down and get out of the basket. He estimated that it would almost take two weeks for them all to get down there. That was even working around the clock to complete the job.

The General was busy calling different bases for more men. Because he needed men for the base that he was going to set up inside of the cavern. He figured that he would need approximately two million men. This way he could set up his base in a very short time. He also knew that it would take him several weeks to get all of this finished. Hopefully he could get it done without drawing to much attention to the public. He then came up with the idea, that if he did draw attention to what they were doing, that he'd spread a rumor that they are just out on maneuvers. At least that would probably keep all suspicions off of him. He told his radio man to call some of the bases and have them send him so many of the new recruits. His radio man was going to be very busy for quite some time. He had over thirty bases to notify. Because each call that he had to make, would take him more than one hour to cut through all of the red tape.

The General then sent word by messenger to the Sergeant in Idanha to tell the nosy people that they have started their war games and that no one may enter. But only if they ask, are they to be told. Then the General had sent twenty-five more men to the south border to reinforce them. This way if anyone tried to get through, they would indeed tail.

The General then turned back to his priority with the pit. The General had also sent several officers down with the men to assist the group leaders with their commands. Each leader was sent three Majors, ten Captains, and twenty Sergeants. They would carry papers with them until they reach their commanders. Then they will hand their papers to their commanders in charge. The papers will state who they are and what their functions will be. This will be treated just like the real military base. The officers went down with the second group of men. They will take the first of the jeeps so that they can meet up with their leaders to discuss what their next steps will be.

The time was 2:00 am. The crews in the pit were being slowed down to almost a crawl. There were so many soldiers coming through, that they had to stop what they were doing every half hour to let a jeep pass them. The crews were trying to finish working on the pipe. Because they only had like one mile left before they could link it up with the Y pipe. In between each jeep, they tried to knock out up to six sections at a time. They figured that this would be the best way to finish the job. Then they had to start on things.

It was now 5: am. The jeeps started to roll in where Eric's camp was. Among the first of the jeeps were the officers that had been sent to him to command. One of my men came over to wake me up. He told me that they had started to arrive. I saw how close they were coming to the camp with their jeeps. So I had some of my men take out a bunch of lanterns and told them to make a runway out of them. Somewhere out of the way of the camp. Then I had them explain to the others on the radio what they were to do.

The General had sent me the following officers to command.
Major Tom Ellison - First Class - Decorated with the Purple Heart - _ Medals of Valor and the White Cross
Major Earl Jones - Second Class - Medal of Valor - and the White Cross
Major George Lucas - Second Class - Medal of Valor - and the White Cross

Captain Jonathon Edwards   Captain Michael Hendricks

Captain Terry Saunders   Captain Larry Potts

Captain Gerald Stone   Captain Henry Wilkes

Captain John Erickson   Captain Peter Boils

Captain Mickey Sanchez   Captain Timothy Andrews

Sergeant Bill Henderson   Sergeant Mike Booth

Sergeant Bart Thompson   Sergeant Carl Jenkins

Sergeant Donald Horsy   Sergeant Hermann Trotter

Sergeant Will Mathews   Sergeant Corey Pines

Sergeant Jeff Bates Sergean   Sergeant Reno Stork

Walter Michaels Sergeant   Sergeant Dane Zimmerman

Phillip Morris Sergeant Tony   Sergeant Paul Edmond

Marsh Sergeant Allen Davis   Sergeant Sully Guthrie

Sergeant Dean O'Malley   Sergeant Wayne Forbes

All of these fine men have excellent service records with the United States Army. I could not have asked for a better group of officers that are under my command.

I called a meeting with them to discuss my situation. "I want you men to break up into smaller groups of one hundred each and help me to explore this cavern." "I want five groups to cover the top levels and the rest to search the lower levels." "Now I do not want you to call me unless you find something of great importance." "When you have completed that, you are to return back here and wait for the rest of us." "Under no circumstances are you to venture off to anywhere else without my telling you to." "Major Tom Elliot, you come along with me and the other men that are left." "I will need you for certain." "Yes sir." "We will explore the very bottom level and see where it leads us." "Sergeant Jeff Bates, you will keep your men here and set up receivers allover the place." "You will call the General and ask him to send down several units." "Then send some of your men after them and start setting them up." "I want them placed under their maximum range for the best reception." "Now we do have quite a while to wait yet for all of the men to get here." "The General will have someone contact us when the last ones are sent down." "Better yet, when they do call, have them wait there and let them bring the receivers with them." "Does anyone have any questions?" "Good, then the meeting is closed." "You can go do whatever you want for a few hours." "Consider this your off duty time."

I assigned one of the officers to overlook the lists of supplies that came in on the jeeps. He was to make sure that we got everything that is on the lists. How he did this, I left up to him, just as long as the job was done correctly. He then hand picked twelve men to assist him. I called the General and told him that I needed rope, block and tackle, batteries, tools, receivers, and whatever else he thought that I may need. He said that I will get all that I asked for and more.

My men where checking the lists as the jeeps came in. The ones that he had checked out, seemed to be in order. He said that we were even getting enough rations to keep us going for about two weeks. That was good news, because I could not tell how long that we would be down here. So I made sure that all of my men were stable enough to handle it.

The General was busy making sure that all of his plans were going according to schedule. Then the soldiers he had called were starting to arrive. So he changed his plans a little. After he had sent down another sixteen hundred men for us, he sent two thousand down for himself, so that they can get started on the new base camp in the cavern. Along with them he also sent down several loads of equipment for stringing up the lights for the caverns and tunnels. He wanted them to get started as soon as they got there. This way when he gets down there, it will already be lit up. When all of our troops finally arrive, the General plans on bringing down all except for a small crew of fifty men to stay topside and protect the camp from saboteurs. This also will keep the main camp open in case that we may have to evacuate the caverns, that we will be able to do so. Each of the main four groups were given a total of three hundred jeeps. This gave them an extra fifty jeeps for putting extra equipment and for taking the necessary samples. The piping crew had finally finished the last tunnel. They then proceeded to seal up the holes around the pipes. That would start up the venting system. Then the tunnels would start to clear up, after a few hours.

Another crew had started to put up some fans on the tunnel ceilings to help draw out the mist. If everything went according to plan, then the tunnels would clear up in about three hours.

The two weeks went by very swiftly and the rest of the men had finally arrived. It would take another four hours to get everyone situated for what they had to do. Something told me to look at my watch. It was already 3:30 pm. It was to late to go anywhere today, so I told my men that we would leave first thing in the morning.

Dale's group had gone another five or six miles deeper. He had his men stop for the night. He tried to radio back to the general, but he was already out of range. The General tried to get Dale on the radio for over one hour, but he didn't have any luck at all. He did not know if anything has happened to him and his men or if they were just out of range altogether. He sat down and went through his notes to see exactly how far Dale was actually in there. The General told some of his men to take some of the receivers and set them up along the way. When they reach Dale, they are to leave the rest and return back to camp. Dale was in the third tunnel to their left. When they got about three miles in, they stopped and set up the first receiver. Then they continued to the next stop. They put up the next six receivers and called Dale. They asked him how much further that he was in. He told them that they only had about four miles to go. They told him that they were bringing him some receivers for him to set up as he went along. It only took about ten minutes for them to reach Dale. When they got there, they told him that the General was wanting to talk with him. They unloaded all of the receivers into one of Dale's empty wagons. Then they had left back for their own camp. Dale called the General and told him what had happened, that they were in no danger, they were just out of range.

The General told him to be sure and get those receivers set up as he went along, to prevent this from happening ever again. He did not want to worry himself to death over something like this, but in either case, it did. He said that it would not ever happen again. That right there set the Generals mind more at ease.

The Captain's men found their way to him without any difficulty. He told them to get a few hours of sleep. Fore they had a very long day ahead of them tomorrow. At 11:30 pm, his men were out like lights. All of the jeeps were lined up waiting for morning. He was sure that he had nothing to worry about since his men were very light sleepers.

The crews were very busy installing all of the new lighting system that was going into the tunnels and caverns. The first set of crews were putting in the electrical conduit in all of the tunnels and caverns. The second set of crews were coming in behind them and running the wire through the conduit. Then the third set of crews were putting up the light fixtures and wiring up the lights. Then there was a fourth set of crews getting the power generators where they are suppose to go and wire them up. There were several generators in each of the tunnels and caverns. If some tunnels had more than one chamber, they would install another generator. The General wanted to make sure that they had plenty of power to cover everything. If some of the generators would bum out, then the backups would carry the workload until they were replaced.

So far, the venting system is working perfectly. Some of the tunnels are almost completely clear. This will make the crews work more swiftly. The electrical crew is also hooking up the power to the fans. Then besides the lights, they are also putting in electrical outlets. This is for the other work that they may have to do in the future. At least then, they would not have to rely on battery powered tools, because they usually were not strong enough to do some of the jobs.

Up on top they are running electrical cable to the highway and tying it into the electric pole. Then they will connect it up to the first of the generators. From there they will split it up between all of the generators.

It was 6:00 am, the General had already gotten up for the day. He called the lab to find out the results of the tests. They told him that after the slime has completely hardened, it was absolutely harmless. Only in its natural state, can it be harmful. They also said that the mist was rich in Oxygen. That is why the plant life was doing so well in the cavern. The General then asked them if there were anything else to report. They told him that there was not. The General then hung up the phone. He called the piping crew up. He told them to go down into the fourth tunnel to run a one inch pipe from the main line into where Dr. Kline is and leave it open. They must run the pipe in at least two hundred feet for it to be effective. This was for the plant life in there. The General then called all of the teams up. He told them that they can take off their safety suits. He then told them that under no condition are they to touch the slime in its natural state. If they need to deal with any of the slime, they are to put their suits back on. All of the leaders were glad to hear that, because they were hot and sweaty inside of those suits. Now all of them can enjoy the comfort of the cool air in the tunnels and caverns.

The time is now 7 am. It was time for everyone to go back to work. Dr. Kline had his men spread out about ten feet apart. He wanted to make sure that he did not miss a thing. He wanted to cover the area with a fine tooth comb. He told his men that at times, some things that are very small, often get missed. He had a small group of men recording all of their findings. Besides that, he also had a man making a precise map from all of their descriptions. This map will also include the locations of each variety of vegetation.

They had discovered that in every two hundred feet, there is a small pool of water. These pools of water seem to be spring fed. He tested the water for impurities and found that there was none at all. This water was the purest spring water that he has ever seen and heard of in his entire life. He told his men that they could drink all of the water that they wanted to. That it would not hurt them at all.

Dale and his men kept going farther into the tunnel. They put up the receivers as they went along. One about every fifteen to seventeen miles. His group has gone about forty miles farther. Dale wanted to test the signal to see how he was coming in, or if he was coming in at all. He told the General how far away he was. The General told him that he was coming in real well for that distance. The receivers were definitely doing their job.

Captain Miller had set out to uncover the mystery of his cavern. First they went down the right side of the cavern. He had his men spread out as far as they could without falling into the slime bed. For the slime bed seemed to follow the cavern. They were able to spread out for two miles, then they went forward. They came to the end of the cavern on the eleventh mile. Then they had to turn around and go back to the bridge. They crossed over the bridge one at a time. For he had a fear of collapsing the bridge all together. They first found out how wide this side was before they continued forward again. He found this side to be five miles wide. They spread out and moved forward to the end. The length of the cavern on this side was fifteen miles long. It took them about two or three hours to reach the end. For they had no idea of what could lie ahead of them, so they just took their time. At the end of the cavern he found a road like area that went up to another level. They all drove up to the next level. They had to see where it went. It was over three hundred feet above the other level. This one was ten miles wide and twenty-two miles long. At the end of the cavern, they found another tunnel and followed it. Then he remembered that they have not set up any receivers, so he sent two jeeps back to set them up. He told them that he would wait for their return.

Over in Eric's cavern, they had separated into groups. They all separated and took a different path. For this cavern was the largest so far. There were many tunnels going from one part of the cavern to the next. Eric thought that they could cover this one before the end of the week. Each of the levels was about two miles square. His men were everywhere. Eric wanted to know exactly how many levels there were, so he drove all the way to the bottom of the cavern. It took him well over four hours just to get there. Once he was down there, he drove out to the middle and stopped. He had one of his men take out a telescope and set it up for him. He wanted it mounted right to the hood of the jeep so that he did not have to get out and set it back up every time that they moved the jeep. This took about another hour to finish. He then started looking through it to count all of the levels. He was barely able to count them all the way to the top. For every level, he had to stop and refocus the lens. He had counted thirty levels in all going up. He then wanted to see how long it was. He turned towards the east and drove twenty-five miles to the wall. Everywhere he looked, he saw the same thing. After he had reached the wall, he had found another tunnel. He told his driver to go ahead and drive on through. This tunnel was about two miles long. They came to an area that looked like an underground lake. He could not even figure out why it was there or what it was for. He took samples of the water to find out if it was fresh or salt water. He knew that in some cases the water would be salt water. He also tested the water for possible contamination and found that it was pure. He also knew that in most cases the water would be contaminated. When he discovered that it was not, it confused him totally. He just could not understand why it was pure when it should not be. They drove around using the power of their search lights to see with. They drove as far as they possibly could go. Then they were forced to turn around. For they had run out of dry land to drive on. As far as he could see, there was nothing else here to be found, but he did make sure that he documented every little thing that he has found so far. They went back to the cavern that they had come from. They went back through the tunnel and proceeded to drive to the other end of the tunnel. Before he left for the other end, he had three of his men take a count of how many sections there were in all. It took them about one and a half hours to reach the other end of the cavern. When they got to the other end, he asked his men how many that they had counted. They told him that there were forty-five in all. He figured that this cavern was about seventy-five miles long. On the other end they found another tunnel. They again drove through. This tunnel was about four miles long. On the other side, they came out into what was a cavern just like the one that they had just left. He had no idea what so ever, as to what they were or what they were suppose to be used as. All he could do was to take an educated guess as to what their purpose was. These two caverns reminded him of something that a type of being would live in. But what kind? This one was much longer than the last one. It certainly felt like it. It took them a whole two hours to reach the other end. As soon as he reached the other end, he again found another tunnel. He decided to go through it one more time.

On the way through, he was hoping that it did not lead to another cavern, like the last two. The tunnel was only four miles long. When they came out on the other side, he was very amazed. Sitting right before him was a huge forest. He could not even see any signs of the other end of the cavern. He thought that maybe this cavern was larger than the last one. He noticed that it was starting to get dark out. He looked straight up above the trees. He could see the sky and the clouds, but how could this be, he thought to him self? There was no breeze or anything else, but yet, the sky was indeed getting darker.

He decided to spend the night right where they are. He instructed his men to set up camp for the night. But he had to get something done first. He sent a small crew back to set up the receivers so that they could keep in contact with the main base. He told the driver to make a drop and continue on to the next point to speed up the process. Then they were to come back as soon as possible.

Seven hours later, his crew had come back and told him that the job was finished, so I called up the General and let him know that we were all right. We just forgot to set up the receivers. I told him about my findings and told him that we are going to stay here for the night. Then in the morning we will continue to search this cavern. He told me to keep in better contact with him in the future. He does not want any people disappearing on him. I told him that I will and ended the message.

I did not really know what to expect in this cavern, so I had some men stand guard throughout the night. I did not want to take any chances on losing anyone. Every three hours I had ten of my men standing guard to protect the rest of us. The hours of the night seemed to move by very quickly. No one really knew that last night was rather long.

It was 7 am and the guards woke everyone up for the day. I asked them all if they got enough sleep. Their reply was yes they did. We all sat down to eat our breakfast. At the same time, Tom and I were discussing our next moves. He suggested that we split up into two different groups to cover this one more swiftly. I of course had to agree with his suggestion. For I did not really want to spend to much time in this cavern. I had the last one on my mind to much and I wanted to get done with this one so that we could go on to the next one.

At _ am everyone was done eating and finished loading up the jeeps. We were finally ready to leave on our venture. As we drove into the forest, I noticed that there were many different types of plants that I had never seen before. I could not even begin to describe them since they were so weird looking. No one could really believe what they looking at. They had no idea of how these plants got here or even why they were here, but they knew that they had to make the best of it.

Eric had his men spread out so that they could cover this one swiftly. After driving for about an hour, they came upon a very large lake. It must have been at least five miles across. He could even see the trees on the other side of it. Here they split up and drove around both sides of the lake, keeping in contact with each other.

Half way around the lake, they noticed the forest was moving away from the lake and turning into a grassy plain. Here they found all types of different kinds of grass. From the fine green grass, to the tall coarse brownish grass. After twenty minutes of driving, they came back to the forest. This side was much thicker than the other side was.

It took them one and a half hours to completely drive around the lake to the other side where they met up again with Tom's group. From there they continued to search the forest until they came to the cavern wall, which was one hour away from the lake. Eric figured that they have seen enough and had everyone one turn around.

Instead of going back through the forest, they took the narrow path next to the wall of the cavern. This was flat and they knew that it would not take as long to get back to the tunnel. In this cavern, Eric had seen at least one hundred kinds of small critters. Three -fourths of them should have been above ground, not underneath of it. The cavern was lit up just like the other two that they were in. The top of the cavern was so high, that it looked like it was not there at all.

It took them two hours to reach the tunnel. There he set up another receiver before leaving the area for good. Then they entered the tunnel and headed back towards the camp. It was time for them to head back and meet up with the rest of the groups. They had seen everything that they could see in here. They had started back towards the first cavern.

It was well after dark when they had reached the others, but they made sure that they had set up the receivers along the way. The only way that they were able to see was by using their search lights. Everyone was getting pretty tired and ready to get some sleep for the night.

The Generals men were busy at work trying to finish installing the new lighting system inside of the large cavern that the General wanted to turn into a military base. He had also sent one thousand men to the cavern where Eric was, to put up some more lighting.

CHAPTER *Three*

D ale's group had already bed down for the night. The next morning Dale's men woke up rather early. They got up at 5 am and prepared themselves for the long day that was ahead of them. They left shortly after they had finished their breakfast leaving behind them one receiver to mark the beginning of the day. They traveled twenty-eight miles when they had come up to the edge of a huge cavern. This cavern was lit up. But there were no signs of where the light was coming from. This was most definitely strange. Where was the light coming from? This was a question that he had to find the answer to. Before him was a huge city like area. The structures stretched out for a very long way. He had no clue as to how far these structures went. They disappeared far beyond his line of sight. After he had finished gazing upon the structures, he thought that he had better give the General a call on the radio. He informed the General on what he had found. He told the General that the cavern was lit up somehow, but he was not sure of where the light was coming from. The other thing that he found was that the cavern was full of these very unusual looking structures with very unusual symbols on them. He could not make out the symbols because he had never seen symbols like these before.

The General told him not to go any farther. That he was going to send down some more men to help cover this area. He told Dale that the men would be there in about three or four hours. Dale told the General that he would wait for the new recruits to get there. The General asked Dale if he could see any signs of life. Dale replied that he could not. The General told Dale to back up at least one mile and wait. This way if anything did happen, Dale and his men would be able to get out of there. Dale said that he would back up. Before he started to back up, He looked around for a few minutes. As far as he could see, the structures stretched on and on. There was no end to them. He could not even see a wall or ceiling. Yet he knew that there was one somewhere out there. The structures went way up in the air stretching out like little fingers. Some were so high up, that he could not see the top of them, but he still did not see any movement of any kind. He told his men to back up very quietly. They backed up for one mile and came to a stop.

The General said that he would be there in a few hours, because he also wanted to see this for himself. Dale knew that he had to wait for a long time, because it took him so long to get to this point.

Dale could not resist the temptation of going back into the cavern. He simply had to see more. He ordered his men to stay put. They were outraged. They saw no reason for him to go back in there without any type of protection. Dale told them to quiet down and listen. He tried to convince them that he would be fine, but they still did not believe him. They said that he was disobeying orders. Dale agreed that he was, but he also reminded them that he was not in the service. He was just a civilian so he did not have to follow anyone at all, if he did not want to. They knew that he was right, but they still did not want him to go in there. They watched as Dale walked off in the distance. His body kept getting smaller and smaller as he walked off. He looked like he was in the book of Alice In Wonderland. Dale did go without his men, but he also did not want them to get Court marshaled either. He knew that he was doing the right thing by leaving them behind.

Dale came back to the entrance of the cavern. He just stood there for a while. He was carefully taking in what he was looking at, but he was not sure if he could believe his own eyes. Then he walked inside of the huge cavern. There he kept walking up to the structures, looking all around him. There still were not any signs of life. Dale wondered who or what had built these magnificent structures. How long have these structures been standing here like this? Another question he had to find the answer to.

It took him over one hour to walk up to one of the structures. He could not find an entrance anywhere. How did they get in or out of there? He looked very carefully for something that might be a key to open it up, if there was one. It took him about one hour to walk completely around the structure while he carefully examined it. He saw no doors or windows. Just a smooth flat surface except where the symbols were. He touched the structure and found that it was hard and cool to the touch. The structure had many different colors and patterns above the symbols. It almost looked like it was carved out of stone. He gave it a smack with his hand. It had a flat dull sound to it. The sound was the same as a rock would have sounded like. He then knew for sure that it was made out of stone. He looked up and studied the area. He also saw what had seemed to be a walkway going from one structure to another. He could see at least four extending from just one level going to each of the other structures in different directions. The fourth one went to what looked like another passageway in the wall where he had came from.

It looked as if it were about two or three hundred feet up. It would most certainly be very difficult to reach. He saw at least three more sets of walkways at even higher levels. The way that these were built, he could not tell if there were any doorways at the top of the walkways. This was most definitely a great find. He was very proud of himself, because he was the first one to discover something so extraordinary.

At the entrance of the pit, the General is sending down hundreds of troops and jeeps. He told them to go down tunnel number three as soon as they hit the bottom. He himself was coming in the first group that went down. He had left Cornel Davis up on the surface to overlook the movement. He was then instructed to get the other base underway. The General took about five thousand men with him.

The call for discovery came in about 10 am. It was now 1 pm. Only twenty-five hundred men had made it down to the bottom. It will take about another three or four hours for the rest to get down to the bottom of the pit.

It took the General about four hours to reach Dale's men. The General got out of his jeep and walked up to Dale's jeep. He asked where Dale was. The soldiers told him that Dale had ordered them to stay put while he walked off to investigate the structures. The General got in the first jeep and moved them into the cavern. They stopped about two hundred yards from the structure. The General got out of the jeep. He got out his binoculars and looked around for Dale, but he could not see Dale anywhere.

The General could not believe that what he saw was so real. It looked like there was no end to all of those structures. He told the men to let him know if they caught a glimpse of Dale. He had his men set up camp until the rest of the soldiers had arrived. The soldiers set up the camp on both sides of the entrance to the tunnel. The camp had stretched out one half mile on each side of the tunnel. There were about four complete rows of tents, but there still is more men coming, so they had to make sure that they had plenty of room to set up the camp without getting into the way of the structures.

The General decided to go look for Dale. He took one jeep with a handful of men. They drove over to the structures where he thought that he might find Dale. They were looking at what seemed to be the find of the century. Dale was out there somewhere looking those over like a little kid. They only had to drive around for about half an hour before Dale finally was spotted. They drove right over to where Dale was standing. The General was furious, but he also knew that Dale was just a scientist. He also knew that a person can never keep a scientist chained up.

Dale told him that from what he has found. The entire area had been abandoned. He still could not find a way into the structures. He then pointed out that there still might be a way to get inside. He told the General about the one walkway that lead right to a passageway in the face of the rock where they had come out of. He told him that the only problem was that it might be to high to get to. For it seemed to be a few hundred feet up. The General told his men to start looking for any passages that they could enter.

It was going on 6 pm. The General called off the search for the night. He told his men that they would start looking again in the morning. The men continued arriving until well after 8 pm. The all settled down for the night. They left guards on duty throughout the night on 3 hour shifts to watch over the camp.

It was 7 am. Captain Miller's men had just returned. They had spent the night sleeping by the receiver, for they had went to bed around 9 pm. They said that they had set up several receivers and they needed to set one up right here. After the receiver was set up, they took off again down the dark tunnel. They stopped about five times while they were in the tunnel and set up the needed receivers. They started coming up to a large opening, so they slowed down very quickly. Right at the opening, they set up another receiver.

It was another cavern. This one was not lit up either, so they had to proceed very cautiously, for they did not know what was ahead. Captain Miller had an idea. He stopped all of his men. Then he turned on his search light. He looked around to see how far away the wall was. He could not see it in any of the three directions that he looked in. Then he told his men to start pulling up side by side, leaving at least ten feet in between each other. After they had finished moving up, he told them all to turn on their search lights. They were to follow the path of their lights. Maybe together they can see something. It seemed to have worked. What they found was just an empty cavern. It only seemed to be a couple of miles long in any direction. The only place that they did not check was almost straight up, so they tried that. About half way up, they saw a large ledge. It stuck out about fifty feet, most of the way around the cavern. Besides the ledge, there were about twenty or thirty tunnel passages. They did not see any way up there. One of the men shined his light behind them. Not to far away from their tunnel was a ramp going uphill to another tunnel. He pointed it out. Before Captain Miller and his men took off, they checked on the other side of the tunnel for another ramp, but unfortunately, there was not one. They also had to set up a temporary receiver right where they were, so they could venture on. Once again they were on their way, heading up the ramp towards the tunnel. Captain Miller stopped again to have a receiver set up. After it was set up, they proceeded on. The tunnel was still going up as it curved around. It did not take to long before they came to a spot where the tunnel had leveled out. There they set up another receiver. Then they left again.

They finally reached what was only the first of these tunnels. It branched off. He did not know where it would go, so he had one of his jeeps follow it to see where it went. He told them that if it went out to the ledge, that they were to wait there until further notice. He soon came up to another tunnel. This time he told his men to stay put. He took this upon him self to investigate this tunnel. For he wanted to see where it went and what lied ahead. He only had to drive for fifteen minutes before he came out on the ledge. Then he saw the other jeep sitting by the other tunnel. He called them over to where he was. Then he called the rest to come down the tunnel that he had come down. Once they got there, that they were to take a left turn to follow him. He again took off and followed the ledge to the last tunnel. When they had reached the tunnel, they entered it and found that they were headed back the way that they had come. He had no idea of what this area was or what it was used for, but he sure wanted to know.

It took them one hour to get back to the main tunnel. It was already half past one am, Captain Miller told his men that they were going to stay here for the night. They set up camp. Then they made out reports and maps of all of the caverns that they had been in for the day. Captain Miller radioed in all the information that he had. He told them that he was going to stay right there for the night so they could finish making their detailed maps. He said that they would see them in the morning sometime. The Kernel told him that it was all right by him. Just as long as they felt that it was safe enough. Captain Miller assured him that it was.

Dr. Kline had reached the other end of the cavern. Another tunnel stared him right in the face. He gathered up his men for a meeting. The only one he had stay behind was his map maker. He wanted him to finish his job up before he enters the next tunnel. It only took them ten minutes to drive through it. They came out into a much larger cavern. This one had a forest in it. It was also lit up from above.

In this forest, Dr. Kline had found all sorts of fruit trees. All of them bearing fruit, ready for them to eat. This is just what they saw before entering the forest. He had some of his men gather up some of the fruit. One of each and every kind. He wanted them for samples to be tested. He gave them strict orders not to eat any of the fruit. For he could not tell if they were safe to eat. There were Apples. Peaches. Oranges. Lemons. Limes. Bananas. Coconuts. Cherries. and many other types of fruit. There were almost any kind you could ever imagine.

Dr. Kline could not figure out what they were there for, or even why they were there. All he could do was to look at the wonders set before their very own eyes. He walked into the vast forest and came up to another pool of spring water, but this time on the other side was a grove of vines with berries on them. They looked like Wild Raspberries. This was driving him crazy.

He quickly ran out of there and back to his jeep. He then called all of his men. He told them to sit down and eat a real good meal. He told them to stay out of the forest until they had filled their bellies full of food. He explained to them that the fragrances of the fruit and berries were making him so hungry. Here they stayed to eat and rest for one and a half hours.

Cornel Davis was keeping everyone on their toes. All kinds of preparations was still underway. Over half of the land that was cleared away had been used up for the needed supplies. They had just sent the bulldozers away. Since they were not needed anymore. This gave them extra land to use for other equipment. Cornel Davis had finished reading the reports and decided to check on the lab. He called up the lab to see if any new results have come up. He spoke to Captain Johnson about their progress.

Captain Johnson told the Cornel that they are still having some trouble figuring out the slime. That it was the only news that they had to give at this time. The Cornel told them to keep working on it. Captain Johnson said that they would. The Cornel then hung up the phone.

Inside the cavern, General Hawsers men are trying to locate the tunnel that could lead to the walkway that they saw. The General had the artists sketch out a picture of this so he could have a copy for himself. He said that one day he would have something to show his grandchildren. Besides the pictures, he would tell them a little story about what he had seen.

Dr. Kline and his men had just finished their rest after eating a big meal. Now they were ready to go back to work. They all went back into the forest trying to get as much work done as possible before it gets dark. Dr. Kline said that now he can handle all of the sweet fragrances without going crazy. He looked at his watch to see how long it would be before nightfall. He only had about three hours left. He went back to where the pool was and walked around it to the other side. Just beyond the raspberry bushes were some grapevines. Then to the left of the vines were some strawberry patches. Everywhere he looked, he was finding different kinds of fruit. This was blowing his mind.

One of his men called him over. There lying on the ground was a thick bed of brilliantly green colored moss. The kind that you can walk on without hurting it. This type of moss usually grows in certain climates. It is so comfortable when you take your shoes off and just walk on it. "Just try to imagine how it would feel if you walked on it," Dr. Kline said. Right in the middle of the moss patch, there was about seven or eight different types of mushrooms growing. I must find out how all of this got here, he thought to himself.

He pushed farther into the forest and found even more amazing wonders. He was already a football field length away from the pool. He had come up to another pool with flowers and reeds three fourths of the way around it. There must have been at least thirty or forty different varieties there. In one part of the pool, lay some lily pads in full bloom. He actually saw a frog sitting on one of the pads. He looked even closer and saw some goldfish swimming about. This was getting to be to much for Dr. Kline to handle. He actually had to sit down on a huge rock for a while.

The most beautiful sight that he had ever seen was over whelming him. Anxiety was kicking in. Some of his men came over and asked if he was all right, but all he could do was to just nod his head yes. He looked at the flowers around the pool, remembering the fruits. Then he looked up at his men and began to let the tears run down his face. He just could not understand why all of this was here. "What purpose was it suppose to serve?" he asked. It was getting close to being dark and his men suggested that they stop for the night, so that Dr. Kline could get his thoughts straight. They knew that this would give him a chance to get better for tomorrow. Instead of going back to where the jeeps were, he and his men decided to make good use of the forest. They all wanted to sleep among the trees and flowers. Dr. Kline agreed to let them do it, for he also wanted to do it. He thought that if he slept among the flowers, that it would do him some good. Besides that, he wanted to sleep here at least one time.

As he sat there staring at the flowers, the light started to fade away. He looked at his watch. It was half past eight pm. He then continued to watch the light fade away. Leaving all that he could see in the dark. He then had his memories left to go by. Still with the tears rolling down his face, he thought of the many different kinds of flowers that were there. The yellow and white wild flowers. The violets,-tulips, roses, mums, tiger lilies, and the bleeding hearts. All of these were now just a faded memory, but there were still many more. The only thing he had left, was just the fragrance of the wild honey suckle that filled the air. It was on the far side of the pool. Oh how wonderfully sweet it smelled, he thought to himself. He kept those romantic memories at hand as he started to lay down to sleep. If only his wife were here. He would show her how good of a time they could have.

Time was flying by as they all slept through the night. The only ones still up were the crews back in the pit. The first and second shifts were already gone. The third shift was working hard as they could to finish up by morning. Some of them got all stressed out from working so hard and had to be replaced.

It was three am. They had completed the electrical tie-ins and turned on the power. Everything was lit up like a Christmas tree. All of the receivers were finally installed. Three fourths of the men were sent to the cavern where the main base was being built. That base will be the staging area for all of the troops. Once there, they were put back to work putting up more electrical lighting. There were a few crews bringing in the generators to be hooked up. They placed them where the engineers told them to. They placed six of them near the right side of the tunnel. Keeping them at least sixty feet away from the tunnel. Then they placed six more on the left side of the tunnel. Yet another crew was bringing in some heavy steel gates to be installed at the caverns tunnel edge. This will prevent anyone from getting in or out.

About four hours has passed. They were still working on everything. The engineers were standing at a table discussing their next move. They were going to light up all of the caverns, one by one. They had no idea of how long it would take from start to finish, but tomorrow they will start shipping supplies into each of the caverns that had already been checked out. Which one they would start setting up, they did not know yet. That is what they are waiting to find out.

There are over one thousand men putting up lighting in the cavern right now. The electrical wire is being put in almost as fast as the lights and conduit are. These men are slowly falling behind the others, but that is to be expected. Then behind them are the men who are tying in all of the wires. Their job will go even slower.

It is just past 5:30 am and the men are still hard at work. They had nearly finished three miles of lighting already, but they were no where being done. They had several miles to go. The time flew by very quickly. It is now 7 am. The troops were waking up Dr. Kline. His men woke up to the changing of the light. He had let all of his men sleep all night with no guards on duty. He felt that none were needed at all during the night. When he was completely awake, he could once again smell the sweet fragrances of the honey suckle. Dr. Kline knew that he had a lot of area to cover yet. For this cavern was much larger than the other one. After they had eaten their breakfast, they had gotten under way collecting samples of almost every plant that they saw.

They sent their boxes to the jeep as soon as they were filled. Four boxes had already been filled and they haven't even put a dent into it. In one area there was a small clover patch. Beside it was a melon patch. They saw three patches in all. Each with about twenty or more different varieties. Four more boxes were filled and sent back to the jeep. They ran across more and more spring fed pools as they went farther in. This was almost like a living museum, the Dr. thought to himself. All of the boxes that they had carried with them had been filled. He sent enough men back to bring up the jeeps.

It took them two hours to get back to the jeeps. They loaded up and drove around both sides of the forest area. The two groups would stop every now and then to collect more samples. It seemed like they were stopping every fifteen minutes just for the samples, but there were many other things to notice also. It took them one hour to get back to the point where they had thought that they left their leader. Each of the men took a box with him. Then they went looking for Dr. Kline. They had found him after walking for about half an hour. They kept going, collecting samples as they went. It took the entire group another two hours to reach the end of the cavern.

Before them was yet another tunnel. The Dr. sent his men back for all of the jeeps. Three hours later, the jeeps came rolling in. They loaded up the jeeps with the sample boxes and then they all got in. As soon as the last man was in the jeep, they all had left. They went in and drove for a short while. This tunnel was six miles long. It emptied out into another cavern. This one was different from all the rest. In this one, you could drive down the middle as well as the sides. They split up into three large groups. The area started out as a forest at first. Then after one mile, it turned into a vast jungle teaming with all kinds of wildlife. He had his men get out their weapons just in case the animals tried to attack them.

There were Lions, Tigers, Monkeys, Rhino, Birds, and much, much more. They were all living together in complete harmony. None of them were trying to hurt each other. It was almost like a petting zoo. Except these animals were full grown.

Dr. Kline had gone down the middle of it all. At a few points there were a few lakes on both sides of him, six in all. The lakes seemed to be about one mile across, each. At one point the got out and looked at it. He passed real close by the animals and they did not do anything. They just let him pass. Right there he saw many types of fish swimming about in the water. He checked the water temperature by putting his hand in. Surprisingly enough, it was not even cold. He went back to his jeep and went on. It took them six more hours to reach the other end, but this time there was no tunnel at the other end, just a plain huge wall.

They had all turned around and drove back towards the main base. He knew that they would not get back until sometime the next day. All of his discoveries were now completed. Dr. Kline was relieved that he did not have any more tunnels to explore for a while. He wanted to get his samples back to the next tunnel. They still had one mile to go before they got to it. He planned on, spending the night in the second cavern. This was the place where they spent last night and he was bound determined to get there. He did not care if it took them half of the night to get there. He just did not want to spend it with the animals.

The Cornel had estimated that it would only take ten or twelve hours to the generals remaining men to him. He then called up the

General and told him the good news. The General told him that he did quite well. This was far better than he originally anticipated. The Cornel had spent the of the night shipping down their men. Once they were down there, they were to take what jeeps that they had. Then in the morning then in the morning they would start sending down the rest of the jeeps.

It was 4 am when the Cornel sent down the last of the men. As soon as the crane brought the elevator back up, they would start sending down the jeeps. He told the operator to double the speed this time. This way they could finish the job three times faster. Instead of only sending down twelve jeeps per hour, they would be sending down anywhere from twenty-four to thirty-six per hour. By 7 am, they had already sent down ninety jeeps. The men were taking off towards the General much faster than before.

After Eric and his men got up, they had taken off for the base camp. He told his men that they would be back that very same morning. Then after they rest up, they would shove off for the last tunnel. He was not sure if his men were ready for that yet, but he was going to find out soon enough.

Captain Miller and his men were already moving back towards the base. He knew that they had a very long way to go. They spent five hours driving and he brought them to a halt. He figured that they all needed some rest. While others needed to stretch their legs. Captain Miller checked over their maps that they made up. It looked like they were over half way back. He was very pleased with the results. They rested for a short while and then took off again.

The Generals men still have not found any new tunnels. He was getting very frustrated over the entire matter. He had Dale take half of the men and go search the other end of the enormous cavern. It was most definitely huge. As Dale passed by some of the structures, he noticed that some of them were so much taller, than the others. They stretched beyond where he could see. The shapes of the structures kept changing. As they drove by, he had two of his men taking pictures of everything. He said that the more information that they can gather up, the more it would make sense in the end. He told them not to miss a thing. Some of the structures were tall, short, and wide. Some were even shiny, while others were dull looking. One of the wide ones seemed like you could fit an entire shopping mall inside of it. The further they went, the more different the structures became. Why did they leave here, Dale asked himself. He was not quite sure that they just left or if they perished. This was another thing that he wanted to solve.

They drove for hours and hours and still have not found the end of the cavern. As far as he could see, the structures continued on, not being able to find a single clue. They passed one structure after another, none of them were the same. Each one of them looked just a bit different. Then something caught Dale's attention. Out of the comer of his eye, he caught a glimpse of an unusual structure. He moved closer to it. He had caught the sight of some carvings on this particular structure. He wondered what it meant.

Was it some kind of message that we ca not understand, or is it just a decoration? He was not sure at all. He studied it for a while. Then he came up with the conclusion that it had to be a message, for there was nothing like it on any of the other structures. At least not like the way that this one is. Why this one? And why right here? Why not over by the tunnel? These are questions that he needed to find the answers to. He had his men take several pictures of the structure before they moved on.

They went about five miles and noticed that they could see a wall. They headed right for it, but it took them three hours to reach the wall. Once they got there, they found another tunnel. Instead of them all going in there, he sent only one jeep. He wanted to see where it went from a different angle. The jeep was gone for about twenty minutes or so. Then he could hear it coming, but where from? It was not behind them. Nor was it to the right of them. He looked to the left. For it was the only direction left. It was not there either. Where was it? Then a tool had hit the ground. He then looked up and there was the jeep.

One of his men was waving his arms around. They were trying to get his attention for about five minutes. Dale took his men into the tunnel. It went up and around to a certain point, then leveled out. When they came out of the opening of the tunnel, they began to see another world. One you could not ever expect to see. These things that he had thought to be walkways, were big enough for two jeeps to fit side by side. With a sidewalk on both sides. This really made him wonder. He drove up to the other jeep and went right on by. He wanted to see inside of those structures, but he knew that he only had a short way to go. After a few minutes, he came up to one. They drove right on in, not even hesitating, even for a second, also it runs upwards and downward. He did not know which way to go, so he got out of his jeep, walked over to the edge, looked down, then up. He could not see much of anything going up, so he decided to go down and see what was there first. He only allowed one jeep to go with him. The others were told to wait for them to return. On his way down, he saw level after level that looked like it was either worked in or lived in. He could not determine the answer, not yet anyway. He figured that he would soon enough find out the answers to all of his questions.

They went down several levels and decided that he had seen enough, so he turned around and went back up. When he got back to the place where he had started from, he signaled for the others to follow him. He then started to go up inside of the structure. They went farther and farther, looking at everything as they went along. Each of the levels were pretty much the same. They had gone up about fifteen levels before they came to a split in the road. He had ten jeeps take the split and find out where it went. He took all the rest and continued upwards. After they went up another fifteen levels, they came to the top of the structure. Here they found another roadway, so he had so many of the jeeps follow each of the paths to find out where they may lead. He then went back down to the first walkway that he had started from.

Once he got there, he had some more men take the different paths. He then went back in the same direction that he was going in before he took the detour. He wanted to see more of this. Everywhere he went, things were always changing. He could not find any two structures that looked the same. He then realized that if they were to get lost, they would not be able to find their way back. After driving around for about an hour, Dale decided that it was time to contact the General and tell him where they can come up. He called the General and told him how to get to where he was.

Eric's group had come back about an hour ago. Then came the Captain's group. The Dr. has not yet arrived. Eric and Captain Miller got together to discuss what they have found and how each one differed from the other. Captain Miller told Eric about the one cavern that was so unusual from the rest. Eric told him that it sounded like it might have been some type of arena. What type, he had no idea.

Captain Miller said that does make a lot of sense. Since it was designed the way that it is, but he still could not figure out what it was used for. Eric told him that he had no other answers to offer him. Then Eric told the Captain about the ones that he had found. Eric told him about the two that were the same in every way. That they were divided up into alternating cubicles, each one about two hundred feet apart. He said that these looked like they may have been some type of living quarters, but he was not sure of that. For the next few hours, they compared and shared notes with each other.

Four hours had passed. The General found Dale. The General told him that he had found the way up there without any trouble at all. The General told Dale to take as many of the troops that he wanted. Because he was going back to the tunnel, where they had come in and wait for the rest of the troops to arrive. The General left all of the troops with Dale and he left for the tunnel. The General then got on the radio. He told the three leaders to come to the cavern where he is and to bring all of their men.

This had upset Eric because he had planned on going down the last of the tunnels, but he knew that he had to go. They had traveled for about two hours and they had come to the mighty cavern. A convoy of over a thousand jeeps came rolling right on in. The leaders met with the General. The General told them to take their men and go search for more tunnels in this cavern. He said that there must be some more tunnels here somewhere. He said that he did not want anyone to come back until they had searched the entire cavern. This made Eric's day. He thought that he would be doing something drab, but this was perfect.

As they all were leaving the area, the General told them to be sure to set up their receivers. This cavern was over sixty miles long and twenty-eight miles wide. Dale had not heard what was said, because he was already out of range, but he still had his men setting up receivers along the way. It took him another four hours to get back to the upper track, but once he got up there, he had all of his men split up and search all over the place. He told them not to leave a stone unturned. They took him at his word.

Captain Miller's team went to the left to search along the wall for the cavern tunnels, if there were any at all. Dr. Kline took his team and went to cover the wall behind the General. They ended up driving ten miles before they came up to a tunnel. Dr. Kline took seven jeeps along with him. He told the others to keep looking for more tunnels. If they find some, they are to keep splitting up until they reach the end. If they do not find any, they are to come back to this particular tunnel and enter it. Then Dr. Kline had left into the tunnel. He followed it all the way to the top, where they had come out on top of the runway.

Here they went over to the first structure. He told the men in the last jeep to check this one out. The others are to keep following him. They drove through the structure and out on the other side. They had to drive about two hundred yards before they came to the next structure. Dr. Kline kept doing this until he himself, was the last one. He then searched all around in the structure, level after level. Everything looked the same. He went up over twenty levels, with a runway at about every fifth level. There certainly was a lot of searching that had to be done. All of the groups had been searching everywhere.

They reported finding twelve tunnels that lead to the structures. There were over thirty thousand men and over three thousand jeeps searching the entire area.

Every structure that had been explored was reported. Their findings were that every level contained a different layout, but they were all empty. Dr. Kline went to the very top to the last runway to find out if he could see the top of the cavern. This was the only one he was able to get close to. He found out that he could see the top, but he could not see if anything was visible, until he looked through his binoculars. He could barely see something that looked like it was moving, but he thought that he was just seeing things. He did not mention it to anyone, for he had a fear of being laughed at, so he just blew it off.

They had recorded over eighteen hundred structures. This took them over five hours to do. They still are not finished. This was just the beginning, but it was getting dark and they had to shut down for the night.

Back at the new base camp, things were moving right along. They had just finished putting up the rest of the lighting that they had. They had brought down another fifty generators. They aligned them beside the other ones on both sides of the doorway. They put fifteen on the left side and thirty on the right side. They held back five generators for emergency purposes. The engineers thought that they had enough generators. Between them all, they should put out over five thousand volts. That should be plenty of power for the entire base and all of the caverns. The next step was to build an area large enough to house over four hundred batteries. These batteries were the size that, were used for electric forklifts. Each one is three feet high by two feet wide and three feet long. All of the batteries will be linked together and tied into the main system. This will be the backup power supply. In case, the main power should happen to go out.

They have already brought in materials for building several parking decks, for military use. The engineers estimated that they can easily build an eleven story parking deck. Each parking deck will be about two hundred yards wide and one quarter of a mile long. They want to build at least four or five of them altogether. Then they need at least ten eleven story barracks for the men. This is all they have planned for the moment. Each floor will be divided into ten sections. Every section will hold about fifty men comfortably. Most of this will take about a year to complete.

Over at the pit, they have completed several levels of steel beams for the elevator to ride on. That is about two hundred eighty feet per day. They are still working very hard trying to finish so many feet a day. They use two foot long steel spikes to anchor the beams against the wall.

Back on the surface, the trucks have slowed down. They are not coming and going like they have been. The crews had been able to get caught up on sending down supplies to the lower level.

The hours of the night rolled on by as though they were only minutes. Two shift changes have been made. The time was going on 6 am. Soon the research teams will be waking up. In the meantime, the Cornel was talking with Captain Johnson at the lab. The Cornel asked him if there were any new developments yet. The Captain told him not yet, but they were hoping to have a breakthrough very soon, but for the time being, they are stuck on a problem and they are busy trying to figure it out. The Cornel told them to keep up the good work. Then he let them go.

The time was now 6 am. The teams were awake and having their breakfast. They were only given twenty minutes to eat. Then they must go back to work. The time that they were given to eat, went by before they knew it. They were off again in search of the missing link. They had spent the good part of the day going through each of the structures, but they kept coming up empty handed like they did yesterday. They had gone through more than a thousand of them. They felt like they were wasting their time, so they started coming down little by little. When the men saw their leaders leave, they too, started to leave. It only took a few hours for everyone to stop and return down below. The General had asked what was going on. They told him that there was nothing up there for them to find. They had gone through more than three thousand of those structures in two days. They said that they had enough.

The General said that he just wanted to be safe and not sorry. They had understood that. This is why they had stayed up there for so long. The General said that there still were other areas to look into. It took them two and a half hours to get back to the base.

Eric had noticed that the unexplored tunnel was lit up. He asked the General what was going on, because that tunnel was not suppose to be lit. The General asked his engineers if they knew something about this. They said yes. They took it upon themselves to light it up, so that when someone goes through there, they would not have to slow down until they get to the end. They said that the tunnel is over seventy miles long. The General yelled at them for going in there without permission. The engineer said that he had over forty men with him. He felt that he did the right thing. The General said that it did not matter if he did the right thing. That he had better get permission the next time, or it will be the end of his career. The General said that it was already 4 pm and there was no sense in going any farther until tomorrow.

Eric, Dr. Kline, Captain Miller, and Dale all got together to discuss their game plan. They talked about how many men they were going to take. How long they thought that the cavern was. They talked about it for three hours. Then they all sat together at dinner and talked about old times. How they were missing their younger years and wishing that they could be young again, even if it were only for a few short hours. They even laughed about some of the women they used to know. They carried on for at least two more hours.

At 9:30 pm, they all went to bed for some needed sleep. While they slept through the night, the crews were busy at work. The engineers had gone with the crews to set up the lighting in the caverns. The engineers wanted the lighting set up a certain way. They even made their blueprints as they worked. They worked on it the whole night through. By morning, they had some of the areas nearly finished.

By the pit, the crews had put another eight hundred feet on the elevator shaft. They had got more done than they originally estimated. They were proud of themselves for getting so much done so quickly.

It was _ am, the troops had got up and ate their breakfast. They had their first hot meal in three weeks. They gorged themselves. While they were eating, the results of the samples came back. The announcement was made. All of the vegetation samples were real and non-toxic. This meant that they had was great. Then all of the water samples were pure spring water and drinkable. Now this definitely had raised questions m Dr. Kline's mind. He still wanted to know why these things were the way that they are. According to his figures, all of the plant life should have been dead, but it was not.

After breakfast, they all gathered around for a meeting. Dr. Kline had told them where they were going next. He wanted them to stay alert and ready for anything. That they did not know anything about the area that they were about to enter. He agreed with the others, that most of the men should go. This way if they came into a huge cavern, they would be able to check it out more swiftly.

The General said that he was staying behind to do some sight seeing in the caverns that he had heard so much about. He told them that if they needed help, to just give him a call and they will come running.

The receivers had been set up during the night, so they would not have to worry about that until they got to the cavern. He also said that Eric and Dr. Kline were the two main leaders. With Eric holding more power and authority than Dr. Kline does. All others were to answer to them. The men had checked over the jeeps to make sure that they had enough fuel and supplies for a long trip. They found that they needed to replenish some of their supplies and took care of it. Then they took their manifests and handed them to the General. The General said that everything seemed to be order and that they could now leave.

They all piled into the jeeps and waited for the signal to go. Eric had control of over two hundred thousand men, but this time they were fifty thousand jeeps instead of twenty-five thousand. Some of the others are empty for bringing back samples. They ran out of room before, because of all the samples that they had collected.

It was 8:45 am when Eric and Dr. Kline got into the first jeep and gave the signal to take off. They went out to the first sub tunnel, turned right and went down the third lighted sub tunnel. They new that they could very possibly have a long journey ahead of them. They discussed many things along the way there. All about what they could expect to see and what they may not see. They had some doubts, but not to many. They did not want to fly down there since they had no idea of what could be ahead. They had agreed that it would not make any sense in risking someone's life, so they went down the tunnel at about 35 mph. They had to much respect for life, to take a life carelessly.

They had gone about halfway, in about two hours. Things were getting tense as they got closer and closer, but they both knew that if they gave up, that someone else could get all of the glory and they did not want that to happen. Eric brought the convoy to a halt. He had spotted some markings on the wall of the tunnel. The markings covered an area four feet wide and seven feet high. They were the same markings that they had seen on the structures in the large cavern. What do they say? What do they mean? These are questions he needed to get answers to. He took pictures of them and went on. They only had about one mile to go. He felt that they were getting close. There it was, the end of the lights. Now they knew that they were there. They slowed down and entered cautiously. This one looked even larger than the last one did. It was full of the same structures with the same markings.

Once again, Eric had brought them to a halt. Dr. Kline got out his telescope and had one of the men mount it to the jeep. Fifteen minutes later, the telescope was ready for use.

As he peered through it, he saw so many amazing things. The markings on the structures were so huge, but they were exciting to look at. He studied the cavern and its contents for a long time. He most certainly did not care how long it was taking, because he did not want to miss anything at all.

After an hour of looking around, Dr. Kline thought that he saw something on the far side of the cavern, but he was to tar away to make it out, it was just to blurry. He told Eric that if he was to make it out, that they had to get closer. Eric asked him how much closer did he want to get. John told him that they need to get at least halfway. Eric said that will be possible.

The trip to what they thought was the half way mark in the cavern, took them four hours to reach. Once again, John looked through the telescope. What he had looked at before was a very large opening in the wall of the cavern, with two columns going to the top of the opening for support. He said that he could not see beyond that because there was a very long tunnel there. John said that he still wanted to get closer for a better view of the tunnel.

Again, they left towards the tunnel. This time they came within three miles of the tunnel. John took another look at the tunnel. "The columns have the same markings on them that are on the structures." "But there is one thing that-is-unique about them." "What is that John?" "Well Eric, the pattern of the markings is totally different." "What do you mean John?" "Instead of the markings running in a random form, they are running in a uniform pattern." "There are at least four to a row from top to the bottom." "Just beyond that is the other end of the tunnel." "I can see some daylight on the other end."

"What is that?" "Am I seeing things?" "What is it John?" "Take a look for yourself Eric." "You are not going to believe it." "What in the world!" "How can this be possible?" "I didn't think that there was anything alive down here." "I didn't either." "Shall we try to get even closer Eric?" "Why not." "This definitely needs a closer look."

They drove the rest of the way to the tunnel and came to a stop. John took another look through the telescope. This time he was able to make out every little detail on the other side. What he had seen, he simply could not believe. "Eric there is movement on the other side of this tunnel." "So what we did see, was not just our imagination running wild." "No Eric, I'm afraid not." "There are so many more of these structures over there." "But they seem to look a bit different." "What do you mean John?" "There are all different shapes and sizes to these." "Wow!" "Just look at that thing move!" "What?" "Look at what?" "Those things are moving so fast!" "We need to get closer yet Eric." "Okay, but we're not taking all of these men with us just in case this turns out to be a trap." "I agree with you Eric."

Eric had all but two of the jeeps back off and split up into two different groups. He told them that he wanted them at least one mile apart from each other and one mile away from him as well. Then they proceeded to move deeper into the tunnel.

CHAPTER *Four*

The opening in the wall itself was one mile deep. They had gone about half way through when they were met by some kind of vehicles, there were four in all. They were also longer than two semi trucks put together. They did not even have any wheels on them. How did they manage to move, they wondered. They had no idea. All of the vehicles just sat there motionless for about fifteen minutes.

Then something start to happen. At the same time, we deployed the men on both sides of us. We told them that no matter what, they were not to fire until we gave them the order. We made that quite clear to them, that if they did fire, that they would be thrown into prison for over ten years. They said that they understood what we told them. The last thing that we needed, were some trigger-happy soldiers.

The first vehicle started to open and some beings were coming out. About twelve of them had come out and stood in front of us. They were a humanoid type of being. They had very tiny ears near their necks. They had what looked like a small nose and a very small mouth. Their eyes were twice the size of ours with one big difference. They had four of them. One set had a funny looking lens cover. The other set of eyes were green with a blue and white center. The lens cover had almost looked like an insect's eye, but we could not say if that is what is was, not without being able to study them more closely. They had a very pale whitish blue color to their skin. We could also see something that looked like gills at the base of their neck.

They stared at us for just as long as we stared at them. On one hand, they had real tiny fingers. Three with what looked like a thumb. Eric had noticed some webbing between their fingers. They had very short bodies. Their so-called feet were similar to their hands. They had four webbed toes. Behind their legs, was some kind of skin that looked a lot like a rudder from a boat. It was also on their backs, but much larger than the ones on their legs. Their head was much like ours with a thin line sticking up about two inches on top and getting larger as it went down their back.

They were not wearing any type of clothing at all, so we could see their entire bodies. They also did not have any body hair like us. They stood about four feet tall. They looked like midgets compared to us. One of them turned around and went back to the vehicle. Then out of the other three vehicles came some more beings. Somewhere in the neighborhood of fifty to one hundred. We had no idea of what was going to happen next.

One of the soldiers asked if more men should come forward. Something told us to say no. It was some sort of intuition to say that and we stuck to it. We told our men to put their weapons down. They hesitated, but followed our orders. About four of them came forward to where we could see them better. We heard a voice come from the background. Where the four were coming up to us. It sounded like it was human, but yet it was not. The voice said that they mean us no harm. As they got closer, they even looked human, but they did not have any clothes or body hair, but all four looked very similar to the others.

The one creature said that they have come from a dieing planet about two hundred thousand light years away. That their planet was in the Telaxian Galaxy. It was destroyed by a supernova. They have been here for seven of our earth years, which was equivalent to two of their years. They have come in peace and wanted to stay on our planet. It said that they would be willing to share their knowledge in return.

Dr. Kline asked them why our planet. It told them that they have passed through many galaxies and have not found a planet that could keep them from dieing. It said that this was the first one they found that could sustain them for the rest of their lives. It said that the four of them used to be human at one time. The others promised them that they would receive knowledge beyond their belief, but in order for them to receive the knowledge, they had to undergo a new body change, otherwise the knowledge would destroy them.

"The four of us agreed to undergo the transition." "We are glad that we did." "We no longer have the health problems that you have." "There are many more of us still here." "Many have agreed to become part of their society as a gesture of friendship and fellowship." "We now possess the knowledge that your people will receive." "The only thing that we ask for is to be left alone."

Dr. Kline asked how many there were. It said that there are about four million in each of five different locations, which they will not reveal. Just in case this one fails. It said that they were prepared to parish if needed. Dr. Kline asked how they were going to get this knowledge. It said that if we would agree to it, that another thousand would join us to teach us all that we need to know. He asked how they got the knowledge. It told the Dr. that their brains had also been altered and enlarged enough to hold and understand how to use it. Dr. Kline said that now he could understand why they did it. He asked them if they still had names. The one talking said that its name is Tylaxor. The other three were as follows. The one on the left was Bluton. The one in the middle was Silvatar. And the one on the right was Signotin. They did not go by their earth names anymore, but they still know who they use to be.

Tylaxor asked Dr. Kline if he would agree to this exchange. He asked how he could. He would never be able to keep them out of here. Tylaxor said that they would hide the entrance from the rest of the world. Dr. Kline said that if they can do that, then he would agree to it. Tylaxor said for us to wait here and they would return with the others.

Eric, Dr. Kline, and their men waited and waited. Finally, after three and a half hours had passed, they saw the vehicles coming. They pulled up close to Eric and Dr. Kline. Tylaxor stepped out of the vehicle and asked them to back up to the rest of their men. Eric asked Tylaxor why. Tylaxor told him that they need to close up the tunnel and Tylaxor did not want them to be in the middle of it when it is sealed. Eric then told his driver to turn around and go back to the others.

Tylaxor had brought over forty other vehicles along with her. After the others were safely out of the tunnel, Tylaxor aimed a device into the tunnel and shot sort of liquid into it. Tylaxor sprayed the liquid into the tunnel for about five minutes. Then Tylaxor backed away from the tunnel. In about ten minutes, the liquid started to grow. It grew until the entire tunnel was completely gone.

As Eric drove up to his men, he told them to stand down their weapons, that these beings were their new friends. They did what he said to them. Eric counted them as they went by. There were forty-seven in all. They covered over one mile in a straight line. After the wall had closed up, you could not even see a crack in it anywhere. It sealed up perfectly. Eric and Dr. Kline went to the front of the line where Tylaxor was waiting.

Tylaxor said that no one would ever know the difference. Dr. Kline said that they were brilliant for being able to hide that entrance. Tylaxor said that they needed to keep their promise about the entrance a secret forever. Dr. Kline gave his word and made his men take an oath of silence to protect them. Tylaxor said that now they can continue onto the center of the cavern. They all got in their vehicles and left. After they had reached the center of the cavern, they all got out of their vehicles.

Tylaxor started to explain that this cavern and the other one are both cities created for the new comers, as a gift for keeping their promise to the Telaxians. "You mean that we are the new comers?" "Yes you are and so are we." "These two cities were created to be self efficient." "The other caverns are for teaching, exploration, and having fun in." "The animal life here is not to be harmed." "That is why they can live in such great harmony." "The food you seek is in the caverns." "All of the fruits and vegetables are yours to eat." "The fish in the waters are also yours to eat, but not the animals." "They are here for you to learn from only." "If you must have red meat, then you must get it from the surface." "There is great power here if you want it." "But first you must learn how to use it and learn from it." "If it is used wisely, it will take good care of you." "This is only the first step that you will be taking towards the New Millennium." "With this new knowledge, will come your future of a new world." "We are here to be your teachers and guide you in the right direction."

Dr. Kline had asked how the caverns were being lit up. Tylaxor told him that the ceiling was made of a clear Telaxian Alumina. It would hold anything since it was so strong. Right above it were lakes. The sun shines through the water into the caverns. He then asked about the slime and what its purpose was. Tylaxor said to him that when the slime is mixed with two other substances, it then turns into a fuel. Then when it's mixed in other ways that it turns into other things. Dr. Kline told Tylaxor about how they made a drivable surface out of it. Tylaxor said to him that we were already learning.

Tylaxor asked the soldiers to wait where they were for a short while, because Tylaxor wanted to show Dr. Kline something over by the structures. On the way over to the structure, Tylaxor continued to tell the Dr. about how many new things are going to come their way. He asked Tylaxor what that meant. Tylaxor looked around to see how far away from the others they were. It seemed like they were far enough away from the entire group. Tylaxor then took Dr. Kline by the hand and lead him off towards his future in the New Era. On the way, he asked Tylaxor what its human name was. Tylaxor said that it used to be a woman. Tylaxor then told Dr. Kline that she knew something about him that no one else would ever know. He asked her how this could be. Tylaxor then started to quote something that only John himself could possibly know.

> My Honey Suckle Rose,
> How sweet you are to my nose,
> Tenderly seeking the softness of your petals,
> As I picked you from the meadows.
>
> Looking at you with my eyes,
> My heart begins to rise,
> Carefully walking as not to stumble,
> So I may be so gently humble.
>
> Then the wind takes you from my hand,
> So effortlessly carrying you throughout the land,
> Soaring in time keeps you on my mind,
> Leaving little or no traces of any kind,
> To whatever reaches, you are to climb,
> The biggest part of my heart goes with you through time.

For I just wanted you to know,
That you were very hard to grow,
Surely you are the one I chose,
To remain as my...Honey...Suckle...Rose.

With the words that he had just heard. Made him stop and think for a moment. The poem kept running through his head as he wondered how this creature had heard this, for he had wrote this poem many years ago for his wife. Then it dawned on him that this creature was actually his very own ex-wife whom had disappeared a few years ago without a trace. He asked himself if this was really true, or had this creature somehow read his very own thoughts. As he turned and looked at it with a weird look on his face. It said, "Yes my love." "It is I, your ex-wife Margaret C. Kline."

From this moment on, he no longer had any doubts about who this creature was, and with that thought, he knew that he was in good hands and that the world was indeed safe.

Tylaxor lead John over to the structures to show him what they have not found yet. On the way over there, she proceeded in explaining why she had agreed to become what she is now today. She told him that she wanted to experience something new. She said that she was very happy that she had made that decision. She also told him that if she had to do it allover again. That she would still do the same thing. That she had no regrets what so ever. That she now was enjoying her brand new life. She also told him that even though she was happy in her marriage with him, that she also was so very unhappy. Because she had grown tired of the same old, routine and she wanted something new. She told him that after her divorce, she did some extensive traveling. Then one day while she was on the road late at night, they had abducted her. Not for evil purposes, but for the learning process of our species.

He asked her if they were able to breed. If so, how were they able to do it. She told him yes they are able to, but she also said that she would show him when the time came. She told him that there were other things that she had to show him were more important for now. Once they had reached the structure, she asked him if he had wondered about the designs and symbols on the structures. He said yes he did wonder about them. He asked her what they had meant. She told him that the symbols tell the story of their travels through space. How long they had been in space, and what planets they had checked out.

It read that they came across over two thousand different life forms. Some of them were intelligent, while others were not. They also visited over five thousand planets in all. The designs were the many life forms that they had encountered, and they wanted a good memory of them, so they had carved them in the stone for all to see. Then she placed her hand on one of the symbols and pressed. A door was revealed as it opened. She told him that the door would stay open until she pressed another symbol to close it.

His men started to get worried because they could not really trust this creature. They had left their jeeps and proceeded to follow him, but he stopped them and told them to wait by the jeeps. They were going to disobey him. Then he told them who she was to him at one time and that he was in no danger at all.

Tylaxor then pressed another symbol from within the structure. The door had closed leaving no trace of it ever being there. She took John down to the next lower level. There she had touched another symbol and all of the structures lit up at the same time. It was an awesome sight. The troops could not believe what they were seeing. From the way the structures were lighting up the entire place, it made the ceiling look like huge star chart. The vast many constellations were of many Galaxies. This was so incredible. John could see it all from the screen in front of him. Then she pressed another symbol and the inside of the structure lit up. Showing all of the different consoles there were. She told John that there is another seven levels going down even deeper into the structure. She also told him that all of the structures have the same amount of levels going down below the surface. In each of the structures, there is one laboratory for every field in science. There were also two thousand hospitals in the entire complex. That they took up three of the lower levels in most of the structures. The hospital in this structure could take care of two thousand patients all at once.

Then she pressed yet another symbol. This time a series of charts showed up on the screen. Showing all of the caverns and the tunnels leading to each one. John asked her about the other caverns and what they were supposed to be used for. She told him about the two caverns that had sections in them. She told him that those two were the first staging areas for the people to live. She said that in a short while everything would make more sense to him. Now he was completely confused. Then she told him about the two caverns that had huge lakes in them. These two lakes are very deep and they connect together in underground passageways. Then there is and underground river that flows straight to the ocean. They use these two lakes for recreation and exploration; also, they feed off the rich plankton that is in the lakes. They use the river to go to the oceans freely. She said that she herself has seen so many new things in the ocean that she never knew was there before.

Then Tylaxor pressed another set of symbols. A low hum could be heard. She told him that this sound came from the power plant that creates the oxygen for everyone to breathe. Then she told him about the caverns with the forests and animals. She told him that this was a living museum. The food in the caverns was also to feed the animals. The animals will not hurt anyone, because they know that no one will hurt them anymore. He asked her how she knew that this was true. She told him that they could talk to the animals just by using telepathy.

John said that this was definitely amazing. He asked her if she could read his thoughts. She said not unless he wanted her to. This was one of the laws. That no one can impose a thought scan on another without his or her consent, and if they do use it without consent, that they can be put to death. She then pressed a few more symbols on the console. John asked her if they ever put any of their own kind to death for imposing a scan on another. She said that there are records of them doing this, but they run back about a couple hundred years.

Then she took John down to the next level. Here he could see a room full of books. Just like a library. She said that they were putting all of these books on crystals so that the people only had to listen to the story. He asked her what crystals. She walked over to the console, opened it and pulled out some white crystals to show him. He said that these were just crystallites. She said yes, but they can store so much information on one. He asked her how this could be. All she said was that the Telaxian's could make the impossible seem possible, that they are so many years ahead of the human race. John could not doubt anything she said after that, for she use to be human herself. He asked her why they do not just read the books instead of listening to the stories. She told him that when they hear the story, that their mind is able to translate it into pictures so that they can actually see it happen.

Once again, she took John down another level in the structure. On this level was the beginning of the hospital. Everything a hospital would ever need is here in the hospital. On this level, he could see rows and rows of beds. Each section of beds was three feet high with the first bed close to the floor. Then they went down to the next level. Here were the operating rooms and the hospital labs. Then they went down to the fifth level. Here was the hospital supply room and supplies. On the sixth level, he saw the largest laboratory he had ever seen. He told her that with this lab, they could almost put an end to every disease known to humankind.

Tylaxor said that one day almost all diseases would disappear. He asked her how she could know that. She told him just to trust and have faith in her. He said that he would try to. As they went down to the seventh level, they were talking about why she took the transition. She told him that now she has a chance to make life easier for humankind. That she had always wanted to do something good for her fellow friends and now she can do just that. They finally reached the seventh level. He saw something here that he had never seen before. This room was ever so large. It must stretch across to the next structure, but there was something different about this particular room. She asked him to follow her and she would show him.

They walked for about what we would say, would be about two city blocks. They had come up to a large square on the floor. She asked him to stand in the square with her. She then stepped on a marking in the square and it began to rise. It rose up six levels towards the main floor of the cavern. Then it stopped. There before him was another large room with about one hundred funny looking types of vehicles. He asked her what they were. She told him that these were Telaxian Buggers. What he would call a shuttlecraft. She asked him to step inside of it with her.

What he saw was so unbelievable. There was a console with two seats in front of it. A large screen was across the entire front end of the craft. As he turned to look at the rest of the craft, he saw ten rows of seats in the back half of the craft. Each row had five seats. Behind the last row of seats was an empty space that they probably used for storage. She asked him to take a seat at the console with her. She turned on the shuttle and moved it onto the platform. She told him to wait there while she moved the next eleven shuttles onto the platform.

It took here about twenty-five minutes to move them all. Then she joined him. He asked her what she was going to do with all of these. She said that these are better than the jeeps, because the jeeps gave off harmful fumes that would eventually kill them all. She said that the jeeps would be stored in that room. Then that room would become a museum. She had also said that these do not use fuel, just pure energy. She said that she would explain those details later, but for now, they had a lot to do.

They proceeded up to the main level. They came up beside the jeeps. The floor of the cavern had disappeared as if it was never there at all. She moved the first one off the platform. Then she asked her mends to move the rest of them. Then Dr. Kline had his men unload the jeeps and park them onto the platform. They were able to get twenty-eight jeeps onto the platform. He told his men to go with them and park the jeeps where they told them. Her friends rode down with them so they could keep bringing up the shuttles. While they were going back and forth bringing up the shuttles. He had his men load the supplies into the back of the shuttles. It took them two and a half hours to bring up all of the shuttles. They headed on over to two more areas where the shuttles were stored. They needed as many of the shuttles that they could get out of the storage areas.

Tylaxor wanted to get rid of all the gas-powered jeeps, for she had a fear that the air could be poisoned. She did not like that thought what so ever. She told John that once all of the shuttles were out, that the jeeps would not be used ever again. He asked her how many that there were in all. She said that there were one hundred for every structure. That there were over three thousand of the structures between the two caverns. The switching took about eight hours to complete.

Then they were ready to go see the General. They only took twenty of the shuttles with them. Each one had two operators. Most of their friends had to stay behind with the rest of the soldiers. They were to prepare more shuttles for travel, at least as many as they could. Then they were to finish setting up the rest of the structures for operation. She then took John and the others to see the General. It only took them fifteen minutes for them to reach the tunnel. Once they entered the tunnel, it took them thirty minutes to come to the fork where they had to make their turn towards the other cavern. It took them five minutes to reach the General.

One after another, they went by the workers. All the workers could do, was to stand there and watch them go by. They were all wondering what those things were and where they had come from. When they had come up to the gates, John had to get out of the craft so the guards would let them in the compound. As soon as the guards opened the gates, John got back inside of the shuttle. They then proceeded to where the General was. All twenty of the shuttles pulled up near the Generals tent.

These shuttles were so fast, that it only took them fifty minutes to get there from the middle of the cavern, which was over one hundred miles away. They all got out of the shuttles and walked over to where the General was standing with his mouth wide open. When he saw the new comers, He had his guards stand ready to fire their weapons. As John came up to the General, he told them that there was no danger, but the General did not believe him. He told his men to surround the new comers. John soon put an end to that. John told his men to surround the General and all of his men. The General told them that if they do that, they would be court marshaled. John then said that the only one to be court marshaled would be the General. John told the General that his men will stay right where they are until he came to his senses and listen to what he had to say. The General said that he would listen to what they had to say. The General told his men to stand down and fall back. John told his men to stand at ease, but to be prepared for trouble from the other soldiers. They assured him that their new friends would be protected. The General brought John, Tylaxor, and four of her friends into his tent to talk about the matter at hand.

John told the General that all of the gas-powered equipment must be moved out of the caverns and returned to the surface. Then instead of the jeeps, they would have the use of the shuttles. Which were much faster and more efficient. The General wanted to know why the jeeps had to be taken out. John told him that the fumes would kill everything in the caverns after awhile. Also that the fumes were dangerous to the new comers health. The General said that he would take care of that, for he does not want to be responsible for wiping out an entire race of beings. He then asked who would be driving the shuttles. John told him that the new comers would be until the men receive their training.

John introduced Tylaxor to the General. He told the General that she use to be his wife. The General just laughed until he heard her speak. Then he shut his mouth. The General said that he could not believe how this could be possible. John continued to tell him that she agreed to be altered to become one of the new races. The General asked if she could speak any other languages. She said that she could only speak English and Telaxian.

Tylaxor then took the General and John along with her to another cavern. All of her friends and some of the men also went with. She took them to the cavern where the lake was. It took them fifteen minutes to reach the cavern. She asked them to wait while they got their skin wet and ate their food. For they did not want their skin to dry out or their bodies to dehydrate. She said that they must return to the water once every twenty-four hours to maintain their health. They went into the water and vanished down below the surface. They were gone for almost one hour. Then they returned to John and the General. John asked how long that the others could stay out of the water. She told him that they also must return to the water once every day. John told her that some of the others did not go into the water. She said that they probably have already been in the water through the underground passage that leads to the other lake. He then asked her what it was like down there. She replied that the next time he could go with her to find out. He said that he would have to get some scuba gear first. The General said that he would put in an order for it along with a couple of mini subs. John asked the General how long it would take the equipment to arrive. The General said that he would have it by tomorrow. John said that he will be looking for it. The General then asked her if that was okay with her. She said that will be fine since they are electric powered. The General said that he would put through the order as soon as they arrive back at the base.

Tylaxor told Signotin to take the General back to the base so he could do his work. Then she told the others to return to the structures and bring back more shuttles to the Generals base camp. The General asked John if he was coming back with him. Tylaxor told the General that John was going to stay with her and discuss a few things over. They followed her instructions.

After they had left, John and Tylaxor were completely alone. As far as they knew, absolutely no one else was coming to the lake until the next day. "What do you think of my new body John?" "I don't know what to think as of yet." "What are those two insect type eyes for?" "They are for seeing in total darkness." "They enable me to see when there is no light at all." "How do you switch between the two sets of eyes Tylaxor?" "I don't." "My brain does it before I can see the difference." "Do you know that we have the power to change you?" "How, I didn't see any machines down here." "You haven't seen everything yet John." "There are still many new things for you to see and experience." "You did not answer my question Tylaxor." "No I didn't." "We need to build it." "You mean that you also possess the power to do that?" "Yes John." "We can even build a portal to go through time or wherever." "Then why didn't you tell the General about this?" "With the way that he thinks.?" "How long can you live for now Tylaxor?" "Well...My life has been increased by two hundred years." "No way,that's just not possible!" "Sure it is John." "I am now a Yearling." "What do you mean by Yearling?" "As I get older, my body will change and my brain will get more powerful." "You mean, yes John, I am in the first of four stages."

"I have been like this for about four months now." "We are allowed to make others like us." "But they must be willing." "Is it painful?" "Oh no, of course not." "You go into a dream state while your body changes." "You begin to dream about everything that your mind experiences." "You see so much and learn at the same time." "How long does the transformation take?" "About one week." "Has it ever failed on anyone before?" "Only when they were just learning how to do this." "They have been changing people successfully for over one hundred years now." "Do you want to be changed to look like us John?" "Wait a minute." "Why me?" "Because you have a brilliant mind and it may not take as long." "Besides, then you and I can be together again." "Wouldn't you like that John?" "Yes I do want to be with you again." "But now I must have some time to think about it." "This is not something that you just jump into." "I still have a life here." "Is it permanent?" "I'm afraid so John." "Once you go forward, there's no turning back." "Well now, that certainly is food for thought." "Let me ask you a question Tylaxor." "Are you happy now that you have a new life?" "Yes I am." "But I'll be even happier once we are together again." "What makes you think that I'll accept this change?" "I know you all to well John." "You're always looking for something new to experience in life." "You definitely got me on that one." "I do look for new experiences."

"I'll tell you what." "I'll give you my answer in about three days." "Besides, we had better get back to the others." "Not yet John, they won't worry." "I want to spend the night with you." "This way I can show you a few things." "Like what?" "If you allow it, I can share my thoughts with you." "I don't know." "This is a bit much." "I really need to think this over very carefully." "There still is something that I haven't shown you about myself John." "What is that?"

"John you know that I am still deeply in love with you." "Don't you?" "Yes, I have known that ever since you quoted my poem back to me after all of these years." "Come along with me John." "I have something very important to show you." "What is that?" "You'll see." "Just be patient with me for a little while."

She took him by the hand and led him inside the shuttle. She then closed up the shuttle and locked the door so that no one could get in. She unfolded the seats in the back of the shuttle. They turned into what looked like a bed.

"John, this is how much I love you." She sat him down on the bed and backed away from him. She began to glow to a bright blinding light. John had to hide his eyes from the light that she was giving off. Five minutes later the glow started to dim and he could see her again. Her body was once again in human form.

"How can this be possible Tylaxor?" "You told me that this was permanent." "Well the powers that my brain has, only allows me to do this once in a while." "It has a tendency to drain away my strength."

"This is only the second time that I have done this." "Is this going to be your shape for now on?" "No John, this is only temporary." "I can only stay this way for a very short period of time." "Exactly how long?" "For about six hours." "Is that long enough for you to share some time with me John?" "Yes, it will be plenty of time." "More than enough." "I had almost forgotten how beautiful you are." "John, you always seem to know what to say." "You always manage to get me to blush." "Well it is true." "You are just being modest."

She then joined him on the bed and they made love for almost two and a half hours. Then the rest of the night, they slept in each other's arms. The next morning John woke up at about 8:30 am. He could see her new body again. During the whole time she was asleep, John just sat there watching her, like he had always done in the past. To him, she was a Sleeping Beauty. Waiting to be waken by a kiss. He only got to watch her for a very short period of time, for she was waking up for the day. He asked her if what he experienced last night was real, or was it her taking control of his mind. She told him that it most certainly was real.

"Do you people choose mates at all Tylaxor?" "I thought that you would never get around to asking me that John." "But I am glad that you did." "The answer to your question is, yes we do." "We only choose one mate." "And that is for life." "Have you chosen your mate yet Tylaxor?" "Is he a descent person." "Oh yes he is John." "Well I hope that he treats you with great respect." "I'm sure that he will John." "He better or he will have to answer to me." "John , You are the one whom I have chosen." "I love you more than I have ever loved you."

She actually saw a tear run down to his cheek when she told him that. With what she had told him, it caused him to make up his mind. "Tylaxor, do you remember asking me last night if I wanted to join you?" "Yes." "Well with what you have just told me, made me make up my mind to join you for as long as we both shall_ive." ""For I too, still am in love with you." "The love I have for you now, had never stopped." "Besides, I have always wanted you back." "I just never thought that it would be like this." "We had better get back to the others before they wonder what happened to us."

They left and went back to the base. They arrived at the base at around 10 am. They went to the General's tent. The General greeted them with a big smile on his face and asked them if they had a good night. John said yes they did. The General then told them that he had ordered everything that they had asked for. John asked him when the equipment would be coming in. The General said that it should be here in a few hours. John asked him if he would let him know as soon as it comes in. The General said that he will let him know.

Tylaxor asked the General if he had told anyone about finding them. He said no, but he was going to. She asked him not to and began to explain why. She told him that the Special Forces would take some of them to experiment on. Then after they are done experimenting on, them that they would start to dissect them. The General said that she was right. They will not stop until they are all dead. With that thought of losing his new friends, he promised not to tell them at all. If they had to know something, that he would tell them that he had found some unusual type of rocks. John asked the General if he could have a few thousand more men. The General told him to go ahead and take as many men as he needs. John and Tylaxor gathered up the men and left for the structures to start work. It took about two hours to get all of the men together for the trip. About forty-five minutes later, they had arrived at the sight where the work was to begin. John had them all gather around to where they could hear very well. Then John let Tylaxor explain the rest. She said that they were going to help build a series of machines that will change people to what she is. That they will be working very closely together with the other Telaxians. That if they had any complaints that they should speak up right now. Then she told them that they have the first choice of becoming a Telaxian and that they would not be tricked in any way. She said that if they can get enough people in the world to accept the new change, that it would save the world from self-destruction. The men said that they need proof that they used to be human. She said that they would have their proof. She spoke to some of her friends in their language and asked them if any of them would be willing to show the men. They said that they would. She asked for two volunteers. One male and one female, preferably a couple who has already chosen each other. Then she turned back towards the men and told them that these two will show them what they want to know.

The two stepped forward and began to glow. They glowed for about five minutes before the glow started to fade. What the men began to see, was two human shaped people standing before them very naked. The men were finally convinced. All fifty thousand of them volunteered for the new Generation. Tylaxor said that five hundred will stay behind to help convince the rest of the groups. The men asked what their new future would be like. She said that their future would be to help the rest of the world make many new changes so that they can live longer. She also said that the world is coming to a new era, and in five years time, they will no longer need to live on the land. For the new change will give them a new source of food.

The next step after all of this is complete was to get more people to come down for their new life. She said they need to build over seventy-five thousand units, with six pods in each unit. She then told them that they would be in excellent hands. That there was absolutely nothing to fear what so ever. Then she divided them up into smaller groups. This way they could complete the seventy-five thousand units in, about two weeks or sooner. They all went straight to work. While the others were working on the equipment, John and Tylaxor went somewhere else.

She wanted to continue showing him around. She took him to the center of the cavern where the largest structure was. He asked her what they call the structures. She told him that they are called Pendomoses. Which means in his language, Pencil Domes. They went inside of the Dome. There he saw all kinds of artifacts that he had never seen before. He asked her what they were. She told him that this was the last know evidence of their home world. They had saved these to remind them why they are here. After he had finished looking them over, they went down to the next level.

On this level, he saw many types of weapons from early man to present day. This room was just full of them. Any kind of weapon you could ever imagine. They ranged from the African Dart Blow Gun to the Missile. He must have spent over two hours looking them over. He asked her what the purpose was for this. She told him that the reason for all of these museums was to remind them all what direction they were headed in, if they stay the way that they are. He asked if the world was really headed for self-destruction. She said that it was and it was her job to change it if she could. If not, she was to save as many as she possibly could so that they could start a new life.

Then they went down to the next level. On this level, he found all types of seeds that were being stored. She said that one day the world would run out of food due to the Planetary Disasters. If all would be lost, then life would perish. Again, they went down to the next level. In here, he saw something that resembled Space Probes. He asked her if he was right. She said that he was. He asked her if they have sent any out. She told him that none of the probes has come back or sent back any information. She said that the probes may have been destroyed by meteors, but they were hoping that one day they will hear something good. She told him that five hundred have been sent out in different directions. He asked her how far that they have gone. She said that they have gone out of this Galaxy and into the next. He asked her what about the planets in this system. She told him that they would sustain life, but there was not enough water on the planets.

She asked him if he would like to see where the probes are. He said that he would love to see where they are. She led him over to a console in the room and pushed a couple of symbols. Then she told him to watch the screen in front of him on the wall. She pointed out where this planet was and where the probes are at during this time. She said that if the probes do not find anything, that they will not send a signal back. Then she turned off the viewer.

After answering all of his questions, they proceeded down to the next level. On this level, he saw what had looked like huge ships. There were only four of them, but they were definitely big. Each one seemed to be longer than six football fields put together.

And at least two football fields wide. He estimated that they were about forty stories high. He asked her how many levels were on the ships. She told him that each one of these ships has seventy-five levels, but the mother ship has three hundred levels. Then he asked her how many people would be on board each one. She told him that they will hold over fifty thousand people on each one. She told him that there were forty-nine more chambers like this one in this cavern. The other cavern only has thirty such chambers.

She then said that their plan was to get all of the ships into space when the time came. She told him that there was enough ships to take everyone in this country. That really blew his mind. He had no idea that there were so many ships. She then told him that there were other areas like this one all over the world. They had enough ships to evacuate the entire planet if needed. He asked her if he could see inside of one, so she took him on a tour of one. The ship was huge. There were so many places to store water. She said that the water aboard the ships would keep them alive for quite a few years. He asked her how. She said that aboard each of the ships is a nursery that does nothing but grow food for them.

She took him down a corridor and showed him the many small rooms. She told him that these were the living quarters. She explained that they could not spend all of their time in the water. Just during the time that they need to eat. He told her that he wanted to see more of the ship. She told him that it would take a whole week to show him the entire ship. She also told him that right now there was not enough time to show him any more, for there were more important things that had to be done. They left the ship and were going back towards the elevator.

He stopped cold in his tracks. He had seen a very large tunnel. He asked her about it. She told him that the tunnel leads to the surface by the ocean. This was the only way the ships can get out of here. She also told him about another tunnel that leads into this one for the shuttles to get out and head for space. Then they continued up towards the top, for she was taking him to another one of the Pendomoses. She explained that in this one was the nerve center for the entire cavern. From here, they could see or hear anything that they wanted to. She told him to look at the screen in front of him. She showed him an example of what she meant. He could see and hear his men talking as they worked hard getting the machines ready for usage. He asked her to leave it on for a while. He wanted to hear what they had to say about this entire ordeal. She agreed that it was a good idea. This way she could find out if they are really worthy of the next step in life.

What he had heard almost put him into shock. His men had said how much respect they had for him and Eric. They said that the both of them were great leaders. That they would also lay down their lives for them. For anyone who respects life as much as they do, is definitely worthy of the job. Tylaxor had heard enough and turned off the viewer. She turned to John and told him that they were worthy of the new life. That they would become better beings than what they already were. Tylaxor and John went towards the elevator and headed back towards the main level. From there they went back to the others.

The next few weeks had passed quickly. The units were finally finished. John had seen everything that Tylaxor had to offer. There were so many new wonders, that he almost felt that he could not remember them all. He had his men gather around one more time. He asked them to think about what was said to them. Also that when the change is made, that it would be permanent. There was no way back. One by one, they said that this is what they wanted. They were looking for a chance to become a better being than what they already were. After hearing that, John had his men enter the units. John and Eric stayed behind to make sure that nothing went wrong. They also wanted to see how the process was done. The units were sealed and monitored by the aliens. The soldiers went into a type of suspended animation. Then the process began.

Tylaxor said that it would take about a week, because this was a slow process. It was done this way to assure their safety. Tylaxor turned to John and said that he needs to call for more soldiers, an equal amount women as well as men. John told her that they were going to need to explain this reason to the General. She said that the General would understand and dream up some excuse for needing more soldiers.

Eric then said that they could say that they found numbers of new tunnels. That they didn't have enough manpower to check them all out. John said that was a great plan, if it would work. The got into the shuttle and went to go see the General. It did not take them long to get there. The General was in his tent like usual. The General told John that it has been awhile since he had seen any of them. He asked where his men were. John had told the General what his men had volunteered for. The General was furious. He said that we had no right to allow that. Tylaxor told the General that it was their right. No one can own them. The General agreed that she was right. He then asked what they wanted. John told the General that they needed five hundred thousand more men and women. The General asked John if they were crazy. There was no way that he was going to send that many soldiers down there. Eric said that there was a way. To tell them that there are over a hundred newly discovered tunnels and that they have no way of searching them all. The General said that was a great idea, but there was no need to contact the Chief of Staff ever again. For in the beginning, he gave him all the power that he wanted. The General said that he wanted to see the men and see for himself that they were all right. He also wanted to make sure that they were in no danger at all. John said that he was welcome to go see them.

Then John asked if the equipment was here yet. The General said that it was in the cavern by the lake waiting for him. The General told them that he would make sure that the women would be here if everything meets his approval, but not until then. John said that this was okay by him, for he knew that things would turn out just fine. John and Tylaxor bid the General a good day and then left for the cavern. They wanted to spend some time together before they continued working.

It only took them fifteen minutes to reach the lake where the equipment was waiting. John looked things over to see if it was all there. It most certainly was. There was enough scuba gear there to supply a small army of frogmen. John told two of the guards to put the sub in the water at the lake. He said that he would wait for their return. John and Tylaxor only had to wait for an hour. It did not take long for the men to get the sub in the water and set up for travel. The guards gave John a rundown on the mini-sub so that he would know how to operate it in the water. After half an hour of learning to operate the sub, John and Tylaxor were finally ready to go. It took them five minutes to get to the lake. The sub was in the water and waiting for John. The climbed into the sub and sealed it up. They made their final preparations before getting under way. Everything seemed to be in order. They turned on the sub and slowly went down under the surface of the water. John told Tylaxor that this was his very first time going under the water in a mini-sub.

She told him that there was absolutely nothing for him to tear at all. Not as long as he is with her. With that reassurance, John began to settle down enough for them to enjoy the trip. John knew that Tylaxor would have to leave the sub in order to eat and get her skin wet again. She took John deep down towards the bottom of the lake where they do most of their feeding. She said that this area of the lake had the richest deposit of plankton.

After another five minutes of diving, they had finally reached where Tylaxor had to leave the sub.

She got into the water and told him that she will be back before to long. She also told him that if he wanted to, he could follow her and watch to see how they feed for himself. He told her that he would follow her so that he could learn more. She left him all alone in the sub, but he was not scared anymore, for he wanted to see exactly how things were done with them. As they approached the area where she was able to start to feed, he noticed that she was starting to swim very differently. She started to swim just like a Dolphin. Man! Could she ever move too! He was amazed at how fast she was able to get around. This really intrigued him. He wanted to learn as much about her new way of life more than he ever did before. Her feeding frenzy only lasted for about half and hour. She then led him a bit deeper towards the bottom of the lake. About five yards in front of them was a large entrance to an under water tunnel. They entered the tunnel and went about two-thirds of a mile. Then she stopped and pointed up so that John knew where to go. He followed her all the way to the top of the tunnel. About five minutes later the sub broke the surface of the water.

He was now inside a small cavern. She came back inside the sub and told John to steer towards the left of the cavern. There he would be able to get the sub onto a small ledge right next to the shoreline. From here, he had to get out and walk to the floor of the cavern. He was completely astonished at what he saw. This cavern was very small, yet, it was lit up to where he could see. He asked her how this was lit up. She told him that the crystals were giving off the light. That these were the crystals that they use to power up their ships. For this cavern is the only place where the crystals will grow. Because the mineral deposit feeds the plankton that, they feed on. Then because of this, they are able to get the nourishment that they also need to stay well. He asked if they were alive. She told him that in a sense of speaking, they were alive. However, not in the way that they knew them to be. For that, the crystals had no sense of intelligence about them at all. If they did, she would be able to sense that herself.

She led John over to a small area on the floor of the cavern and stopped. This area was soft and somewhat mushy, but it was not wet. He asked her what they had done to this area of the cavern. She told him that they needed a personal place to go when their mates wanted some tender loving care, so they created a few small areas like this one, for them to go to be alone. John asked her if the original aliens ever did this. She said no. "They don't get embarrassed like we do here on our planet." "But in time we will also become just like them in every way." "We don't lose all of our behaviors that quickly." "It takes about a full year for that to happen." This is why she wanted him to become like her so quickly. So that they can mature together.

She asked John to sit down on the floor of the cavern. He asked her why she wanted him to do this. She told him that he would know soon enough. She reached out to him as she wanted him to take her hand. After he had taken her hand, she began to glow again, generating some heat in the process. He did not know if she was going to get any hotter. So he tried to let go of her hand. However, she had a real good grip on him and would not let loose of his hand. After about ten minutes of glowing, she started to get dim again. She asked him why he tried to let go of her hand. He told her that he was not sure if the process was going to burn him. It was just that he got scared. She said that there was nothing for him to be afraid of, since that was the hottest that she would ever get. That is why she would not let go of his hand. She then sat down next to him. She began to hug and kiss him very gently.

Now he understood why he was there. She wanted to make love to him again. This time they spent about three hours making love to each other. After they had rested for about half an hour, John asked her how the others made love. She told him that on the male, a small tube would extend from the belly button. Then the tube would work its way into the womb. She then told him that the nipples on both get very hard during the process of mating. Then the nipples would grow to about one inch in length and diameter. Then they could suck on each other's nipples to start the fertility process. She said that the process takes about four hours to complete. If everything goes right, they would give birth to a little one. She also said that this was a violent process. That the male and the female could not separate, until the process is complete. However, once the process is complete and if it is successful, the male would be able to pullout of the female with the embryo attached to the end of his tube. That process takes about another six hours to complete. Once the baby is fully developed, it will let go of the male and his tube would go back inside of him. Then both sexes would be developing milk in their chest areas to feed the baby. For the baby needed milk from both parents to grow and be fully developed. This was the only way that the baby could get enough nourishment to survive. For each parent has different vitamins that the baby needs in order to grow.

John asked what determines the baby's sex. She said that the potency of the milk from the male determines the baby's fate. That the male has a vitamin called Trufolia. The stronger that it is in the male at the time of birth, would determine the sex of the infant. If the male has enough of the vitamin, then the baby would become a male. Otherwise, it will become a female. He then asked her how they would know which sex the baby is. She told him that the baby's tube would start to develop on the inside. After about two hours of nursing from the parents, the tube would start to extrude from the baby during feeding. He then asked her why he did not see any babies or little ones anywhere. She said that during this time, the parents stay inside until the baby is fully grown, which takes about one month of nursing around the clock.

The baby will nurse on one parent for about two hours at a time. This will give each parent enough time to go eat and build up enough strength to feed the baby. He asked her if this was painful in any way. She told him no. That it was not painful for either parent.

He asked how long the tube would stay out of the baby. She said for about three days. Then it goes back inside of the baby. For after three days, the baby will be about three feet tall. Then in the final three weeks, the baby's growth rate is slow. That it's full size would be only five feet tall. This was very hard for John to grasp on to. He had no idea that it took both parents to feed the baby. However, in either case, this was not going to change his mind about becoming one of them. For his love for her was much too strong for him to let go of her ever again. Besides that, he was extremely glad that she had chosen him to be her mate once again. However, this time he knew that it would be for the rest of their lives. For as long as they both shall live, he knew that he would always have a mate to share his innermost thoughts with. He decided not to hide his thoughts from her any more. That she could read his mind any time that she chose to. She thanked him for that and told him that she would honor him in the very same way. Once his change was complete. Then they both knew that they would be as one forever.

John told her that he did not want to leave this cavern for a couple of days. Tylaxor said that they could spend at least two days there. Nevertheless, they could not spend any more than that.

Because she had an obligation to check, the units to make sure those things were going according as planned. He said that he did not want to stay there any longer than that. For he too wanted to check on things to see how they are coming along. John said that right now was their time to get to know one another again. That he wanted to know everything about her and what she has been doing in these past few years. She told him in the past few years, she had been doing some extensive traveling around the country. That she has been sight seeing and meeting all kinds of people. She said that she had made all kinds of new friends, but now she may have to leave them alone and never try to see them again. John asked her why. She said that they might never understand what she has done. They do not have as much of an imagination as what she does. He said that they do not need to have one. That if they are real good friends, that they would understand what she did.

She asked him if he could deliver a letter to some of them. He said not personally, but he would send a courier to do the job. She said that she wants them to come and visit with her. He said that he could send a team to pick them up and bring them all here. She said that would be great. Then she could be caught up with what is happening out there with the world. John said that as soon as they get back to the others, he would see to it. Tylaxor thanked him graciously. She said that no one else would have done that for her at all. He said that was because they might be afraid of a leak to the outside. She said that she could prevent that from happening with her friends. He told her that she would have to.

They spent the next few hours talking about the old days that they had together at one time. She told him that in a way she misses the old days. But then again, she now enjoys the new life that she now has. John said that he understands how she feels. He knows that it must have been hard for her to just give everything in life up. She said that it was. However, she was ready for the new change. She said that she was glad that she did do this. John said that he knows.

He asked her how often she could change back and forth between the two forms. She said that she was told that she would only be able to do it once a week. However, she has never put it to the test. He asked her if she minded taking the chance to see. She said that she would try. She stood up again and started to glow. It took a little while longer to complete, but she was able to do it. He asked her how she felt. She said that she felt just a tad weak. However, other than that. she felt just fine. John said that he won't ask her to change to much. Because he does not want to take a chance on losing her. She said not to worry about her dieing. Because that was not going to happen. He was glad of that. He told her that he wanted to make love to her one more time before he goes into the unit. She said that she already knew that when he asked her the question. For she also wanted to do this before he goes into the machine. They spent the next two hours making love to each other again. This time he put all of his feelings into action. He did not spare any strength at all. He said that he wanted to remember this moment for the rest of their lives. She told him that she always remembered every time that they had spent together.

She asked him if he would make love to her one more time before he changes. She means in her new state. He asked if the were possible. She said that it was. However, they would never be able to give birth to a baby that way. He said that he would try that tomorrow sometime. She said that she just wanted him to get a chance to see what it was like before he does go into the machine. After they had finished making love, they talked for a little while longer before going to sleep for the night. He told her that he wanted to go back into the ship to explore a little more when they get back. She said that after she checks on everything else, then she would take him back aboard the ship. He said that he would like to make a day of it, if he could. She said that they probably could. He said that it would be great to further his knowledge of the ship as well as the people. He wanted to learn as much as he possibly could before he becomes one of them. This way he will not be shocked in his dream state. She said that the machine prevents that from happening. John said that he did not know that. He kissed her goodnight and they went to sleep in each other's arms. They spent the whole night holding onto each other.

They woke up around 8:30 the next morning. John said that he wanted to go for a swim with her. She said that was a very good idea. Therefore, he went to the sub and got out the scuba gear for himself. After he put it on, they went into the water and went for a swim. She took him around to some of the places where they feed and explore. She showed him a couple of hidden treasure spots that the pirates had at one time. He could not believe how they got this far under water. Then she showed him a few of the other caverns that were private to her kind. They all looked pretty much the same. They were all lit up by the crystals. While they were in the cavern, he asked her how the treasure got way down there. She told him that was due to an earthquake. He asked her how they had found it. She told him that they found something shiny in the water when they were exploring and went to investigate it. She also said that this was part of their museums now. This is something for them to see when they go exploring. Because they really do not want to get bored down there with nothing to see except the rocky cliffs.

He said that was completely understandable and that it was definitely a very good idea. He asked her how long it would take them to get to the ocean. She said about two hours by sub and only twenty minutes if she took him. He said that before they go, he wants to take a couple extra tanks along with him so he does not run out of air. She said that would be a good choice. Because she could forget that, he does not breathe the way that she can. They took a couple of tanks and placed one in the middle of the tunnel floor and the other one at the edge of the tunnel on the ocean side. He had about fifteen of air left in his tank, so they did not go very far away. She took him a mile in only five minutes. She was able to swim quite fast. She showed him various different sites that she has seen before when she went exploring. She wanted him to see as much as she did before.

He looked at his tank flow meter. He only had five minutes of air left. He showed her and she left him there. For she went back for the other air tank. Without him, she was able to swim even faster than before. It only took her four minutes to go after the tank and come back. He could see her coming back with the other tank. He started to take off the first one and then she helped him put on the second one. He now had half an hour of air to spend. They went even farther out than before. She showed him what it was like to be a fish in water. This was something that he could get used to very quickly. He liked everything that he has seen so far. During the next fifteen minutes, he had seen so much of the ocean that he had never seen before. Everything was so beautiful down there and he loved every minute of it. He signaled to her that it was time for them to go back to the cavern where the sub was waiting for them. She took him to where the third tank was laying and helped him put it on, leaving the other tank behind. It did not take to long for them to return to the sub. She asked him how he liked the trip out to sea. He told her that he enjoyed every minute of it with her. He commented on how much he had seen out there and how beautiful it really was out there. He only had what the television showed him to go by. What he had seen was far better than any program that the television could ever show.

Then she asked him if he wanted to try making love the way that she is now. He said that he would try it out. After all, he wanted to see what it was like. He asked her what he was supposed to do. She told him just to lie down and relax. That she will do it all. After he lay down, she got on top of him and inserted him into her belly button. As soon as she got part way down on him, her body just took over and sucked him up inside of her. This created a powerful urge on her part. That in turn had driven him straight up the wall. The feeling was so great, that he let out a huge scream of passion that just increased her sexual behavior. The more that he was turned on, the more violent she became. This lasted approximately three hours, draining all of his energy. However, not harming him in any way what so ever. After her body had released him, she asked him if he was alright. He said that he was fine and then he passed out for about an hour. She sat beside him, watching over him as he slept. When he came to, she again asked him if he was okay. He said that he was. He asked her if it would always be like that. She said that it would probably get more intense than what it was this time. She asked him how he liked making love this way. He said that it was definitely a new experience. However, he was not sure if he could handle it like this all the time. At least, not with him being human. However, if she liked, he would try it again. She said that she would love that. She then said that next time it would be easier for him. He said that would be a relief. He went ahead and got dressed. He told her that they should check in with the others and see how they were doing. She said that she thought that he wanted to spend another day alone with her. He said that he did, but he just cannot get the men out of his mind. She said that she could understand that feeling. For she was feeling that way herself. She said for him not to worry about his men. Because she knew that, nothing was going to happen to them.

She said that she wanted him to make love to her one more time before they return to where the others are. He said that he would because of their love that they have for each other. Besides that, he really enjoyed the strange feeling that she had put him through for that period. He got back undressed to keep the feelings between them the same. There was nothing like being dressed in private when your mate does not even wear any type of clothing. He wanted the both of them to feel comfortable with each other. They had spent the next few hours discussing the artifacts that they both had seen so far. He said that he was amazed at what her kind has found and preserved.

It was going on 6:00 pm and she asked him how he was feeling. He told her that he was feeling much better now that he had some rest. She asked him if he was ready to try again. However, this time he knew what to expect. He prepared himself the best way that he knew how. This time before he got on top of her, he decided to tease her for a little while. He wanted to see if he could get her to react the same way without him entering inside of her. After trying that, he found out that it only gets her started to be aroused. It just was not enough. He got on top and let her take over. He tried to keep up with her, but he could not even come close. She was just way to fast for him. This time they spent a good two and a half hours making love to each other. Again, before they had finished, he let out another scream of passion. After it was allover, they spent one hour talking about how they enjoyed their new experiences. Then they lay down next to each other for the duration of the night.

When they both woke up 8:30 am. He told her that while she is out there feeding, that he will get dressed to leave. About one hour later, she returned and was ready to go back. They got back inside of the sub and went back to the caverns edge where the temporary dock was set up. He tied up the sub and they got into the shuttle. From there they went back to the cavern where his men were in stasis. It took them about forty-five minutes to get back there.

The General was still checking out the situation with the men. He was asking if he could watch them come out and ask how they are feeling. He said that he should go back to camp, but this was more important to him right now. Therefore, he decided to wait out the next two days. Carefully watching the machines and his men to make sure that nothing went wrong at all. For he felt that these men were like his very own children. In addition, he was worried about them all. He even watched as they changed form, little by little. Still asking questions about the process and how it was suppose to work. He even asked them if they were going to share this technology with the rest of the world.

Tylaxor said that if the world can show her that they will not hurt them, then yes they would share some of it with them. However, if they mean to cause them some harm, then no they will not share any of the technology with them. The General said that he cannot speak for the rest of the world, but if it works, then he'll do what he can to protect them from the rest of the world. Tylaxor said that was a very reasonable explanation and she will accept that for an answer.

The next two days went without any problems of any kind. The men started coming out of the units one by one. They were all newly changed beings. The General asked them how they were feeling. They told him that they have never felt this well in all of their lives. He said that this was remarkable. That he had never seen or heard of anything like this in his entire life. Moreover, he has seen so many new things being developed every single day. He asked that he was convinced and that when he gets back to the base, that he will call for more soldiers. He said that he already has over two million men here. Therefore, this time he will call for five million men and women. However, mostly he will send for many more women than men. He just does not want to draw to much attention to himself or this area. He said that everything goes well, that they will be arriving within the next two days. However, it will probably take over three weeks to get them all down here to safety.

Tylaxor said that she was very thankful for his honesty and cooperation. That she will never forget what he has done for them all. That made the General feel very happy that he was able to do something for the good of humankind. With a big smile on his face, he got back inside of the shuttle and went back to the base camp. It took him twenty-five minutes to reach his camp. Nevertheless, he finally made it back there. He immediately got out of the shuttle and went into his tent. He got right on the phone. He called a few of the bases and told them how many people to send him. He asked for fifteen thousand men and thirty-five thousand women from each of the bases from around the country. He told them that he wanted them here right away. They all obeyed his command. For he was the only one in charge of this operation. He also told them that if they had to take them out of training, to do so. Because he wanted a total of a hundred times the people that he had asked for from each one in the beginning. Therefore, the bases had to keep in touch with each other to make sure that his demands are met. The General then sent word back to Tylaxor saying that the new recruits will start arriving in two days. That if she wanted more men in the meantime, he could send her as many as she wants from his base. She sent word back along with several shuttles to pick them up. He sent her over two hundred thousand men. He thought that this would tie her up for awhile.

They started arriving within the next couple of hours. Shuttle after shuttle came in. There were more men than she was equipped to handle at one time. However, this was all right to. For she had a plan to tell them all at one time about what they could expect to see in the future. She even had her witnesses standing by to back up everything that she was going to tell them. Therefore, if there were any discrepancies, the men could vouch for her, in her behalf. Then if there were any who did not believe what she says, could wait until they can see for themselves.

The ones, who did decide to go ahead, got prepared to enter the units. She had them strip down and climb into the units. Then the units had been closed up and turned on. The men shortly fell into a very deep sleep. Then the machine started to lower their body temperature to about sixty degrees. This was to keep them in a suspended state for the full week.

The rest of the men were told to make camp and come visit their mends while they were in the units. Tylaxor wanted them to see the changes that the others were going through during the process. Then Tylaxor, John, and Eric got into the shuttle and left to go see the General in person. Twenty-five minutes later, they had arrived in front of the Generals tent. They got out of the shuttle and went inside to see the General. They knew that he was quite a busy man. Nevertheless, they still wanted to speak with him. Tylaxor thanked him for his understanding kindness. The General told them that the troops would start showing up as early as tomorrow. John said to send them down as soon as they start to come in. Then the three of them left again. Back to the structural caver where everything was going on.

The General called up the lab and asked Captain Johnson if they had made any new progress. The Captain said that they have not been able to break the ice on this new substance. The General told them to pack up everything that they have and bring the entire lab to the caverns. He told them to bring all of the personnel. The Captain said that they would do as he said. However, they will not be there for two days. The General said that would be fine. Then he hung up the phone. Captain Johnson could not figure out why the General had ordered this. Nevertheless, he was sure that they would find out when they got there.

The General then called up Cornel Davis and told him to let him know the minute the new troops arrive. Cornel Davis asked when they were coming. The General told him as early as tomorrow morning. Cornel Davis said that he would notify him when they do get there. Then the General asked Cornel Davis how the repairs were coming along. The Cornel told him that they were done with the repairs. The General said that was excellent. The General then hung up the phone once again. The General then went over to one of the shuttles and asked the new comer if he would take him to see Tylaxor. He said yes he would. The General stepped into the along with three of his men and they left. Three quarters of an hour later, they arrived where Tylaxor was. They greeted her and John. The General wanted to see how things were coming along. They escorted him over to where his men were inside of the units. They seemed so peaceful lying there so motionless. He asked them if they were sure that his men were in no danger. Tylaxor said yes, that they were in the best of hands. He had looked like he lost his best friend. Tylaxor told the General that he had nothing to fear. They are quite safe and no harm will come to them.

"When they awaken, they will be a new race with new lives to live." "For they are your future." "You can become one too, if you wish." "Then you can relive life to its fullest," said Tylaxor. The General told her that he was too old and that he had cancer. That he only had a few years left. Tylaxor told him that they can fix that when he enters the unit. "It takes away all of the diseases and makes immune to them as well." "Then it injects the serum into the body as it changes." "You won't feel anything at all." "If you like, you can stay here and watch the whole process as it happens." "These units are equipped with an advanced warning system that makes the adjustments before any harm can come to you." "If that doesn't work, then we change it ourselves." "This is why we monitor all of the procedures." "When they come out of the units, they will need about six hours to get their strength up to normal," said Tylaxor.

The General said that he wants to stay with his men. However, as far as he goes, he would have to think about it very carefully. He wanted to make sure that he was not going to miss anything in life, as he knows it. "Some of us have been known to live far beyond their two hundred year life span," Tylaxor said.

Twenty-four hours had passed and the Cornel was trying to locate the General. A shuttle pulled up to where the General was waiting. Two of his men got out with a radio and approached him. They told him that the Cornel was on the line. The Cornel told the General that his fleet of troops were here. He told the Cornel to start sending them down below and have them wait. That he is sending shuttles to pick them up. Then the General asked Tylaxor to have her people start taking the shuttles to pick up the troops. He told two of his men to go with and wait there until all of the troops were loaded up. In addition, he wanted them packed in very tight. This would make it easier on their new found friends. Then he sent them on their way to the pit. About three hundred shuttles had left to pick up the troops. Two hours later, the shuttles started to arrive and unloaded the soldiers. They were looking all around them as they got out of the shuttles. No sooner than they got out, the shuttles had left to pick up more soldiers.

In the meantime, the General, John, Eric, and Tylaxor were standing there as the soldiers lined up in columns. Tylaxor handed a small device to the General and told him to speak through it. She said that it will be heard allover the cavern. He thanked her for being so considerate. He then told the troops that the four of them are their commanders. That they will follow their orders and no one else, what so ever. Then he told them to listen to what Tylaxor had to say about their future. He then handed the device back to her. She told them all about what had happened to her. That she was not only glad, but honored that they had chosen her to become one of them. She showed them her entire body, turning and speaking at the same time. She told them that this also could be their future. She asked them to go over to the units and look in on the ones that are already in there. Explaining to them that these men all volunteered to become the new generation for a new life. She also told them about the life span that they would have along with all the knowledge that she now possesses. Next, she told them that when enough people become the new generation. Then and only then, will the door to the elders be opened. She then explained what languages they would be able to speak and understand along with the ones they already know. She then had one of her people take a count of how many people were in this trip. He got on the platform and raised up high enough to take a computer count. Then he came back down. He told her that there were fifteen thousand. She then turned back to the soldiers and assured them that absolutely no harm will come to them. She also told them what her human name was. They asked how they could be sure that she used to be human. She said that she would prove to them who she was. Right before their eyes, she started her change back to a woman. She said that she was taking a chance on doing this again so soon. For it could take her life. She showed them her whole body once again. So that they would believe in what she told them. They then said that they believed her and no longer had any doubt about her existence. She then asked if any of them wanted to have a new life. If so, to step over to the units and disrobe. About twelve thousand of them walked over to the units and disrobed. The others said that they would back up Tylaxor in what she will say to the others. After they had disrobed, they were put into the units. Then the units were closed up and activated.

One half hour later another fifteen thousand showed up. They were lined up and told to wait for the rest of the troops. Then the General said for them all to look around in this cavern until the rest were here. He said that he will call them and let them know. In the meantime, for them to have a good time exploring the cavern. The troops kept arriving for the next three days. After the last load of soldiers had come in, the General called the rest to come back and line up into columns. He told the last of the first group to come forward and face the rest.

After Tylaxor had gained her strength back, she began to tell them what she had told the first group. Moreover, the last of the first group was facing them. If she tells one lie, that the first group will let them know. The first group also saw what she used to look like. It took about two hours for her to explain everything to them. And another three hours for them all to see the ones who already volunteered to enter into their new life. She then told them that there was only enough room for another one hundred forty-six thousand to enter the units. The others would have to wait until the units were empty.

The others had got curious about what she had said. They walked over and looked in on the others once again. They had noticed that some of them were showing some signs of change. While they were waiting for the new ones to come out of the units, the soldiers went exploring the cavern. They had seen so many new and unusual things that seemed so unbelievable. They were also discussing the many possibilities between themselves. However, in reality, they could not begin to understand how this could possibly come about. They spent the next three days exploring; eating and sleeping while they waited. They also could not get the possibilities out of their heads. They spent much of their time discussing between them what it would be like to be one of those new ones.

The announcement came that the units were opening up and they were ready for more of the volunteers. The ones who wanted to do this went over to the units and disrobed. They climbed into the units and were sealed in. All but two thousand were filled. Then some more came over, disrobed, and climbed in. Soon all of the units had been filled up, they had several thousand people undergoing their new change in life.

As the days went by, the General had the rest look in on those already inside of the units. Therefore, they could see what they looked like. He told them that if they had seen it all, that they might change their minds and go ahead to do it. The General asked Tylaxor how many more people she would need. She told him that if he could come up with three million more, then maybe the door would open up again. He said that he would see what he could do for her. He then left for the base. The General came back two days later. Tylaxor told him that thirty-five hundred were about to come out of the units. He had his men gather around to help them out, two men to a unit. Then he wanted them to take the others and lay them down on the beds.

One by one, the new comers were waking up. However, they all were very weak. Therefore, they were helped over to the beds and left alone for the next six hours. General Hawser told Tylaxor that he has a total of three million men and women coming in. They are being sent to the base camp area and the other two areas to wait until notified. He said that they will be coming in for the next two weeks. He then said that in order to keep from tying up her people, that some of his men should be trained on how to operate the shuttles. She said that this would work out just fine. This way her people can take care of the units. She had five hundred of her people take two thousand of his men and train them. She said that within one hour, they would be able to operate the shuttles without any trouble.

They went over to the structure and went down to the seventh level. They walked over to the elevator and went back up six levels. They got out two thousand shuttles that they would need for transporting the troops to the cavern. Within six hours, all of the shuttles were out. The men were being trained on how to handle them. To make things go much faster, there were four students to each of the five hundred shuttles. They were trained in the other half of the cavern. Each one has to spend half an hour driving. Two hours later, they all came back. The General and his men had left for the base camp. The rest of the men were ordered to stay right here. After the units were thoroughly cleaned, Tylaxor said that she was ready for the next group. After seeing that they were in no danger, they went to the units. They disrobed and climbed inside. The units were then sealed up. Soon they were sound asleep and starting their changes.

Six hours later the new ones were fully rested. They now were ready to start living their new life. John asked them how they feel with their new minds and bodies. They all said that they feel great, better than they had ever felt. He said, "Good, then let's go to work." "We need one hundred thousand more units built and ready to go in a week." "Do you think that you can do it?" he asked. They said sure they could, and they got busy on building them. Everyone was so busy trying to finish this huge project. Some of them slept while others worked on the units. However, none of them ever forgot to go for their swim and to eat their plankton.

In the other cavern, the soldiers had started to arrive. They were being taken to the designated caverns. Since the elevator was completely finished, they were able to bring down three thousand at a time. By the end of the next week, they had brought down all of the soldiers. Another plan had been thought of. Instead of putting the soldiers in the other caverns, they were to be moved straight to the main cavern. So they moved them all again. This way they can talk to them as they arrive and see for themselves in what to believe. So far, they have not had any trouble in convincing any of the troops to undergo the new change. They had figured out that by the end of the fourth month, they would have over eight million new comers. I hope that the door will open so they can find out what they are to do. Especially where they are to go. The three leaders decided to be the last ones to undergo the new change. In case, the door does not open. At least this way they will be able to get more troops down there. Time flew by quickly as they worked. Only some of them were afraid to enter. However, eventually they did. At the end of the fourth month, the door did not open. So the General went back to work on getting more people to come down. He told Tylaxor that he would try to get five million more men and women, even if he had to get them out of prison. He asked her that if he did get them out of prison, would the machines change their minds as well. On the other hand, would they remain to be evil. She said that the machine would change them to where they will fit in. That was part of the system that had changed them all. He told her that he was going to get the ones that were only minor criminals. That he did not want to take a chance on the killers. She said that was the better choice of the two ideas. He then left to put all of this into action.

The new ones were spreading throughout all of the caverns. Therefore, they could experience their new abilities. Many of them had found the water to be so exciting. They loved the way that they were able to breathe and move about in the water without any scuba gear. The other part that they had liked is that they can swim as fast as or even faster than a Dolphin. Therefore, they explored the very depths of the lakes. They found them to be over a mile deep. They saw so many new wonders. Tylaxor gave them all schedules to keep. They followed her orders with no complaints. They said that she was more than bur to them all.

The General came back a few days later. He Informed Tylaxor that he managed to get another five million people. However, this time there was a price that he had to pay. Some of the Government leaders wanted to see what they were doing down here that required so many people. Tylaxor said that was all right because the machines would take care of any problems that might arise. He asked her what if they did not want to be changed. She said that no one has ever refused the opportunity yet to become like her. He said that there always was the first time. She said that he was right of course. She told the General that if they cause any trouble, that they will seal up the cavern so no one can get in. He told her that the people would start arriving tomorrow morning for the next six months. She said that would work out just fine. She wanted them brought straight to her. He told her that it would be done.

For the next three months, things were moving along quite well. Then on the first day of the fourth month. some of the Government Officials had shown up to see what they were doing. The General had taken them to see Tylaxor. Therefore, that she could explain all of the details to them. When they had seen her, they were very shocked. They wanted to take over the entire operation. She told them that they could not take over anything without being changed into one of them. The Officials said that she was nuts and that she could not even begin to stop them. On the other hand, they will not be able to stop her either. She began to show them what they were doing and why they were doing this. They said that they want the technology that they now possess. She told them that this technology was only for their race and not anyone else's. She asked if they wanted to become like her. They said no. She said that they must leave. They told her that they would be back with more forces than they had ever seen. She said that she would be right here waiting for their return. The Officials were steamed. The General took them back to the entrance so they could leave. As they were on their way back up to the surface, the General got Cornel Davis on the phone. He told him not to let them back in ever again. He then told him that if they do return in force, for all of them to get on the elevator fast and get down below. The Cornel said that he would take care of this matter. After the Cornel was done talking with the General, he called up both outposts. He told them that these Government Officials were to be treated as hostiles if they ever came back. Also that they were to notify him immediately. They told him not to worry. That they had everything under control.

The next two months went by without any problems from the Government. Then at the end of the third month, the Cornel received a call stating that there was a very large force coming his way. He was told that their arrival time would be one hour from now. The Cornel called in all of his outposts and told them to hurry. It only took them all ten minutes to get there. Now they all had to wait for the elevator to return. The elevator came back up five minutes later. The Cornel told them to get on the elevator, on top of each other if they had to. They only had to fit eight hundred people on the elevator. Another fifteen minutes had gone by and the elevator was filled up. The Cornel grabbed all of his paperwork that he could carry. He set fire to the rest of it. He backed up about twenty feet away and watched to make sure that the shack went up in flames. Then he got on the elevator and started down towards the bottom of the pit. This was the very first time for them all to go down and it seemed very scary to them. They were half way down and the Cornel decided to call up the General. He told the General that the Officials were on their way here and that he needed some help. The General told him that help was on the way.

Tylaxor heard the conversation and took her shuttle along with her. Hers was the first one in line to go. She told them to catch up when they could. She was the first one there and they all were waiting in the tunnel. She passed them up and went into the pit. As soon as she got there, the elevator had started going back up. Some how the Officials gained control of it.

Tylaxor then got out the device and aimed it up into the entrance of the pit. She shot a liquid up there and the pit began to seal up very quickly. It sealed up so fast, that the elevator motors began to short out. Then the shuttle door opened up and Tylaxor came out. She said that it would take them about two years to dig through all of that rock. The Cornel asked how they were going to get back out. She told them not to worry because now they were going to be part of them. He did not understand what she was talking about. However, some how he knew that he was going to find out. Some of the men got into her shuttle while the others waited for more to come.

Fifteen minutes later, two hundred more shuttles showed up and all of the soldiers were loaded up inside. Another half hour passed before the last soldier was aboard. Then they all were on their way to the cavern where they were going to meet their future. The General was not too far behind with the rest of the troops. In all, there were over two million soldiers heading for the new earth base. It took a full week for the last shuttle to pull in. Now they were all there, present and accounted for.

The General and Tylaxor persuaded all of the people to undergo the new change. All of the units had been filled. They had about two million people left in waiting Tylaxor told some of her people to take some of the shuttles and seal up all of the old passages. Then open up some very short ones, linking all of the caverns together. Then they are to remove the vent pipes from the walls. This is to put moisture back into the caverns so they do not have to run back to the water every day. She said that it would probably take three or four days for the mist to take over the entire area again. The General asked her how they could see in the thick mist. She said that their eyes are made for seeing right through the mist. That is one reason why they have two sets of eyes. Both sets work together and not separately.

The General told her that he would welcome the new change. Because he decided that, he was not ready to die yet. She said that she welcomes him warmly. Then she turned to John and Eric. She asked them if they were ready also. They both replied with a yes. Once again, she made her speech to the remaining people. She told them that the new life that she is offering is many times better than their old ones. She told them that all of the people that they see used to be just like themselves, even herself. They said that they would not refuse a chance like this to become something that will live for quite a very long time. Plus to be able to think and speak like a human being. They thought what a wonderful life they could have.

The next month had gone by and they all were now changed into new beings. The mist had taken all over the caverns about a week ago. Now they do not need to run to the water for moisture. However, they still had to return to the water for their food. The following week, they reactivated the pumping system to bring their food right to them. They had to set up many large tanks to hold a fresh supply of water with plankton in it. This way they just had to get in and swim about to eat. They will continue to do this that way, until they develop a way to put it into containers for storage.

Tylaxor told the people that it was time to bring up the rest of the shuttles. Then she wanted to prepare the ships that were deep underground for possible space flight. She had many of them loading up the valuable seeds that have been stored away. She had others start gathering up the food plants and placing them into the storage compartments aboard the mighty ships. She also had others even gathering up all of the animals and birds of every kind. For she did not want to leave any of the creatures there to perish. She wanted to give all living creatures a chance to live instead of leaving them behind to die inside of the rock when it starts to close up.

She said that the ships would house over fifty thousand people. That each one is over seventy-five stories high, two football fields wide, and eight football fields long. Each ship will hold about six to eight hundred shuttles. Then she went to see if the door had been opened up yet, and it did. There before her, stood her creators, the elders. They told her that they were getting ready to leave this planet. That it was too dangerous for them to stay here. The humans simply will not leave them alone. She said that they were making plans to leave also.

They told her that they were the only ones who needed to leave. She said no, not any more. She had a very bad conversation with some of the Government Officials. The elders understood her reason for wanting to leave and they are welcome to go with them. She said that they would be ready to leave in about three weeks. The elders said that they would wait in space for them. Then they all parted.

CHAPTER *Five*

T he door once again had closed up. However, this time it was for food. She and her people got things ready as quickly as they possibly could. Nevertheless, they had to make sure that they were completely stocked with food and water. They transported as much the water and plankton as they could. The other thing that they made sure of was that the plankton growth machines were working perfectly and fully operational.

It took over two weeks to prepare the seventeen hundred ships for space. However, at the end of the third week, they were ready to take off. They took one final day of recreation to take in all of the sights and memories that they were going to leave behind. Many of them went to the ocean through their underwater passageways. They wanted to see as much of the ruins that they could, as well as the sea life itself. At the end of the day, they all returned to the cavern to make final preparations before taking off. After that, they all gathered around and said a few prayers.

Dear Heavenly Father,

Please guide us and protect us during this special time as we flee a world that no longer understands us. We ask you to forgive us for not staying here to help the rest of the world. We also ask you to help us to continue to help keep the plants and animals healthy and alive. We do not know how long that we are going to be in space. Therefore, we are also asking if you would guide us during our flight to find a kind suitable planet in which we could live. We thank you Father for taking time out of your busy schedule to listen to our special prayers. Amen.

They boarded the shuttles and headed for the ships that were deep underground. They followed the secret hidden tunnels that would take them down to their ships. Since these tunnels were very long, it took them two hours to reach the opening of the huge caverns. They sent out signals to the ships as they approached the docking bays. The massive doors opened so they could enter. Once they were aboard the ships, they fired up the engines and prepared for take off. One by one, they taxied over to the runways that lead to their freedom. They followed the underground runways until they came out just above the ocean and headed for deep space.

Ship after ship rose up out of the ground. Like a train without tracks or steam. The followed one another in a straight line. When they broke free of the earth's gravitational pull, they met up with their elders, who gave them a new lease on life. It only took three and a half hours for them all to leave the planet. One hour after that, they reached the rest of their friends. Slowly they started to link up to create one enormous ship. They began linking together side by side until they had fifteen across. Then the ships started to link up from end to end. Until they had fifty in a line for each of the fifteen across. Then more ships began linking up, connecting the first four together like building blocks. Ship after ship followed behind the next. After the first row was completely linked on top of the others, they kept linking up until all four levels were completed. Totaling twenty-four hundred ships. Then the mother ship which was five times larger than the rest, linked up on top completing the formation. All of those vast ships become one enormous space craft.

This craft was forty-five and a half miles long by almost twenty miles wide and seven hundred twenty-eight stories high. The mother ship was over three hundred stories high by itself. The linking up took about three earth days to complete. Once they were all together, they sent a signal back to earth causing a machine to accelerate the growth of the rock. Within five hours, the entire underground caverns were completely gone. All encased in rock. They had to do this to keep the humans from getting their hands on the technology that they did not deserve. They raised up their force shields and had moved on looking for a suitable planet for their new lives. With all of the ships linked together as they are, ten fold had increased the force shield. Not even an asteroid can penetrate it. They were starting to approach light speed and were leaving their home far behind. They were moving out of the Galaxy, away from the sun, out into deep space.

They have been traveling through space for two months and were approaching a planet that may hold some possibilities of becoming their new home. They slowed down and prepared to enter an orbit around a planet. A probe was launched down to the planets lower atmosphere to collect data. They want to find out if there are any signs of life on this planet. It took thirty minutes for the probe to reach the lower atmosphere and start sending back the needed data. So far the returned data showed no signs of any type of life forms. In addition, the data showed that part of the atmosphere has an unusual nitrogen level. With the nitrogen level as high as it is, they decided to look for another planet in which to call home.

They recalled the probe and left the planets orbit. The course had been set for deep space on their original heading. It takes the mighty ship only one hour to reach light speed. Off in the distance, one more planet had been spotted. This one was much larger than the last one they had just left behind. They estimated that it would take about two weeks just to reach this planet. During the voyage to the next planet, Tylaxor and John decided that they needed to spend some quality time together. They wanted to go check on the animals to see how they were doing. On their way there, they were discussing the many possibilities of what the planet could be like.

She asked him when he was going to change his name. He said that he was throwing around a few of them around in his mind. However, he was not sure of which one he wanted. She asked him for one of these names. He told her the name of Truax. She told him that she really liked that name. Because it meant, someone with great authority and knowledge. He told her that will be his new name. She told him that she was proud of him for choosing this particular name.

They finally reached the outer area where the animals were. However, this was just one of the areas where the animals were put. For there were many more animals than what they had space for in just one hold. All together, there are about six different holds that contained the animals. It only took them one hour to get to the first hold. They entered the hold and went walking among the animals. Among the animals was such great feeling of peacefulness. This was something that they both looked forward to. They used special powers to speak with the animals. Truax asked them how they were feeling. The animals told them that they were happy, but they missed the open outdoors. Tylaxor told the animals that they were searching for a planet that they all could call home. The animals asked what was wrong with the old one. Tylaxor told them that the old one was headed for self-destruction. That humankind is on the verge of destroying the entire planet and they do not seem to care. The animals told her that they understood and that they will be looking forward to a new home. After that, Truax and Tylaxor bid them all a good day and continued on to the next hold.

In the next twelve hours, they visited all of the holds where the animals were. Now that they made sure that all of the animals were doing just fine, it was time for them to get some special quality fun. They headed for the hold where the plants were being kept. Upon entering the hold, they saw that the plants were still a bright green. This is very much what they both had hoped for. They walked over to the wild Honey Suckle. The smell of the flowers were so sweet. It most definitely set the mood for them both. For the next four hours they were busy going through their mating ritual. Now that they both were the same type of beings, the love making ritual was very violent between them. Nevertheless, neither one would ever harm the other. After they were done, they spent the next two days talking and walking around the ship.

On the forth day, they returned to the others in the control room. Upon their arrival, they asked if things were running smoothly. The others replied with a yes. Tylaxor asked how close they were to the planet. Mintok told her that they still were about nine days away from the planet. However, their heading was still right on course. She told them that they were doing a fine job and that she was proud of them all.

The nine days had passed very quickly and they were pulling into an orbit around the planet. Since this planet was so large, they decided to send down four probes instead of just one. This way they could cover the entire planet in three days instead of two weeks. This planets atmosphere was almost perfect for them. However, they discovered that some sort of creatures already inhabited this planet. They had no idea of what they were. Nevertheless, they were going to find out. For they needed to know if these creatures were harmless or dangerous. Tylaxor sent three shuttles down to the surface to check out these creatures. She wanted to know as much about them as she possibly could. When the shuttles had reached the surface, they did a low fly by to study them before confronting them. What they discovered had disturbed them greatly. For these creatures seemed to be a violent type of conqueror. This is not what they had in mind for their own future.

After making their report back to the ship, they were recalled. Tylaxor said that this was not for them. When the shuttles were safely back aboard the ship, they left orbit and continued back on their heading. Planet after planet, they either ran into beings that would be a danger to their life or the atmosphere was bad to their health. They had been traveling in space for over one year and passed through one and a half Galaxies. They have not yet found a suitable planet for which they can live on. Nevertheless, they are not going to give up. They have enough faith that they are sure that they will find one. It is only a matter of time before they succeed. Tylaxor assigned a new crew to take care of the animals. She decided to replace the other crew to give them a break for a few months. Then they will go back to work taking care of the animals again. For she wanted to make sure that the animals were well cared for so they don't starve or kill each other. These people will be like a security blanket for the animals. She also assigned certain ones to manage the well-being of the plant life. Because if they should happen to run out of food, they will need another food source. Moreover, she does not want to become what they had just left. For if they do, they may lose all of their special abilities that they were blessed with. Besides that, their teeth are so tiny, that they would not ever be able to chew any kind of meat. The sole purpose of bringing along the animals is to try to create a brand new world out of one that does not have any of its own.

They had kept sending out probes to search the Galaxy for planets that might be suitable for them to claim as their new home. However, so far they have not had much luck in finding one. The planets are either dead ones or full of poisonous gases that would kill them in a few minutes. Some of them were even inhabited with deadly types of creatures or beings that will not ever accept them at all. Nevertheless, they still keep searching for the right one. Some day in the future, they may find what they were looking for. However, who is to judge of whether they do or not. For not even they can predict their own future.

Ten years have gone by. They have passed through five extremely large Galaxies and nothing has been turned up. With all of the advanced technology that they possess, they cannot seem to find a suitable planet in which to live. Yet they seem quite helpless in their effortless search for a new home. They had to move some of the animals around to different parts of the ship because of their population have grown ever so much. They wanted the animals to feel like they have a good home until they can find a good planet. They gave the animal's free roam of certain parts of all the ships and the animals understood what they have been told. They also understood the fact that these beings have given them all a new chance in life. To not only be free from any type of slavery, but also to be friends with each of their species. For they have been promised to be given all the nourishment that they need to survive in a friendly atmosphere. The next thing that they had to take care of was to relocate several plants to different parts of the ships. The plants have grown and multiplied so much, that they were starting to be over populated in the areas that they are already in. They put several of the plants in large storage holds that have been adapted for their special needs. For the people knew that if they did not take care of the special needs of everything that they have uprooted from their home, that they would eventually perish without much of a trace of existence. Therefore, they took excellent care of all the needs that all of the living things had. This then had brought peace and harmony between them all. Plus if their own food supply should in any way become unfit for consumption, that they would have to turn to eating the fruits and vegetables in order for themselves to keep living. This is one thing that they keep reminding themselves of. In addition, when they think of the worst, it in itself worries them to no end.

Another eleven years has gone by. Still not even a trace of a habitual planet has come to their attention. They just could not understand why they cannot even find one little planet that they could call their home. They had passed many planets. Some were large and some were small. However, in all reality, there just were not any that they could begin to claim.

They were beginning to near the end of the twelfth Galaxy. Through the help of the probes, they knew that the next Galaxy was even larger than all of the rest that they had passed through. From the way that the information looked on the screen, that the sun was five times the size of the one, that their original system had. This got their hopes up very high. For they knew that this system could very possibly contain several types of habitual planets. They were hoping to find one planet that would be perfect for their kind as well as for the plants and animals. However, they were still a full year away from the next Galaxy. The water supply that they had originally had plenty of would be gone in about for years at the rate that everything is multiplying. Therefore, they came up with a plan to feed the plants and animals the juiciest fruits along with some water in order to cut down on the consumption of the water supply. For they had to try to stretch out the water as far as it could possibly go to keep them all alive for a few years longer. They telepathically got the animals to agree to this for their increased survival. The explained to the animals that if they could not get their cooperation, that this huge ship would become a tomb for all life aboard. That this would happen in a few short years.

The people noticed that some of them were starting to go through some changes in their appearance. This was something that they were not told when they were changed from human to Telaxian. The changes that they have noticed were as follows: 1. their heads have grown about inches larger. 2. Their mental powers had increased to where they could start moving things by concentrating on it. 3. Their fin like skin on their backside is starting to shrink just a little bit, but more firm. Nevertheless, this new power makes them a bit sleepy when they try to use it too often. Therefore, they try to refrain from using this new power to much.

Tylaxor had called a meeting between the leaders of the other ships that were still under her control. Truax, Eric, General Hawser, Captain Miller, Dale, Cornel Davis, Captain Johnson, and Major Ann Frank were some of them. Eric announced that his new name is Tuluxor. Dale chose the name of Mytrox. Captain Miller has chosen the name of Matrix. Major Ann Frank announced at the meeting that she has now chosen the name of Mytroxaterian. The others said that they have not yet found names that they want to go by. However, before to long they hope to have one. The meeting was called because of the noticeable changes that have been happening allover the ship. She asked the other leaders if they had noticed any changes aboard their own ships. The answer was yes they did. She said that she was never told that these changes would ever take place. Truax said that the reason that she was not told, could be the fact that they did not know that this would happen. Tylaxor asked Truax if there was anything to worry about. Truax said no, not at this particular time. For the changes may be part of their new evolution. That the fact may simply be that, they may become something even greater than their elders ever thought of.

Tylaxor said that this definitely answers her question quite well. She then asked if they should go speak with the elders about this. Truax said that there was no need to bother them at this time. Not until they notice even more changes. If there are going to be any at all. As time went by, they were getting closer to the next Galaxy. Nevertheless, they were still at least a few months away from the next Galaxy. The population has grown by only one third. They have made a unanimous decision not to have too many more newborns until they are able to find a planet to live on. Because they have the fear of becoming extinct in space if they populate too quickly. Therefore, they came up with a plan to only have ten newborns a month. They all have abided by this rule for the past twenty-two years. This is the only reason that they have multiplied so slowly.

This month was Tylaxor's and Truax's turn to make love and try to have a newborn for themselves. They went off to their favorite place on the ship. They ended up in the cargo hold where they were keeping the plant life. They took turns speaking in English and soon went the Telaxian Language. They told each other of how much they loved each other as they started their love making ritual. Since they both decided to stay in their new form this time, they are not able to kiss to turn each other on. However, they are able to suck on each other's nipples to start the process. As they do this, their internal organs start to become highly active. Her belly button hole starts to get a bit lose and moist waiting and wanting him to enter. Then she starts sucking on his nipples to get his donor tube to come out. As it does, it comes out to about twelve inches. Then it starts to leak a secretion. Then he starts to work it deep within her womb. As it works its way in, her internal organs sucks it all the way in her. Not releasing it until it has done its job in finding the egg to insert its sperm. They both get very violent during this whole process. For they are locked together for a few hours. Once he finds the egg and fertilizes it, then and only then, can he withdraw from her womb. They do not hurt each other in the process at all. However, they are bumping and rolling all over the place. The closer he gets to find the egg, the more intense and violent they both get.

Finally after three and a half hours, he reaches her egg and fertilizes it. His tube then latches onto the egg and pulls it out. Withdrawing back into him. The egg will stay there until it reaches the newborn stage. Then it will push itself out into the mothers hands. She then cradles it up to her nipples that are already sticking out about two inches. This will allow the baby to get enough milk until the father has regained his strength. Then the father will take the baby up to his nipples and let the baby suck on him. For both of the parents have to give the baby their own special blends of milk in order for the baby to survive. They must do this around the clock for about three weeks until the baby reaches full-grown adulthood. The father possesses the one key ingredient in his milk sacks that the baby needs in order to grow. Without the fathers milk, the baby will die in three days. The one key ingredient that the male of his species carries, is a vitamin called Trufolia. For without this vitamin, the entire species would eventually cease to exist. Therefore both, the male and the female must mate for life.

The whole birth process takes about one month all together. The baby sucks on each of the parents for two hours at a time. Then the parents get to rest and eat for one hour at a time. They keep repeating this throughout the entire time that they are with they baby. Once the baby reaches adulthood, it will no longer have any ties to the parents. Their baby turned out to be a male. They gave the baby the name of Trulaxator. Who was named after both of them.

The month has gone by very quickly and Trulaxator was getting ready to go his own way. He told his parents that he was very thankful for them bringing him into their lives. That one day he will return to show them his new mate. Then he will go about his own way and they will never see him again. This may sound cruel, but this is the way of their lively hood. This is the way that it has been for over three thousand years and they were not going to challenge that custom. At least not yet anyway, for they wanted to wait until they have reached their new home first. They were told that this custom has worked quite well during all of those years. Moreover, they thought that this was the best way for now. They bid their son farewell and went back to their stations for work. During the next few months, they have encountered two real bad and long meteor showers. Each one lasted for about two or three days. The meteors kept pounding the force shield. It held up just as it was suppose to.

Mytrox and Mytroxaterian have finally gotten together and wanted to spend some quality time together. The two of them thought that they would never find a mate. However, they both were surprised that their wavelengths were both the same. They asked permission to go and have their turn at mutual romance. Tylaxor told them that since this would be their first time together, that it was completely all right with her. They both thanked her and left for the hold where the plants were. It seemed that all of the people liked the plants for their mating rituals. For some reason it seemed to trigger some type of sexual sense that helps get them started. It took them about one hour to reach the hold. Nevertheless, they found it without any problem. Once inside, they chose a spot among the wild Honey Suckle to perform their mating ritual. They both agreed that the fragrance was very pleasing to their senses. She asked him which way he preferred. The human side of their new form. He said that he has never tried their new form, so he voted for that. She told him that was an excellent choice. For she also wanted to try that. He started caressing her body to activate her belly button. However, it did not seem to work. Therefore, he tried to play with it. That did not seem to work either. Then he decided to go right for her nipples. Finally, he was getting somewhere. She started moaning and groaning like a wild woman. Then he noticed that her buttonhole was starting to get very wet. Therefore, he started to play with that and she stopped him. She told him it was his turn to get turned on and she started to suck on his nipples until they were fully extended. She continued to suck on his nipples until his tube was completely extended. Then she stopped and started to insert it within her. It only went in about two inches when her insides took over and sucked him all the way in. The sucking power began to drive them both wild. They made love for about four hours. His tube was finally let go and withdrew from her with the egg attached.

During the next few weeks, they were busy feeding the baby. On the second week of feeding, they were able to tell the babies sex. This baby turned out to be a female. This was because his Trufolia was not as strong as it could have been. However, they both knew that they needed females to increase the population. After the child reached adulthood, they gave her the name of Mytroxator. Who was named after both of them. Mytroxator told them both that she was very thankful that she had such loving parents who decided to give her a life. Then she went on her way to create her new life as a caring individual among the working class.

After watching their child walk off into the world, they both returned to work at their stations. For they probably would not see each other for at least one year unless they reached their new home first. The year had gone quicker than they thought it would. They had sent out ten more probes to search the new Galaxy. The size of the enormous sun is much larger they thought. There should be quite a few planets in this solar system that do have life on them. I hope that the probes will find something here. At least that is what they are hoping to find. Because they do not think that, they will be able to survive very much longer. For the water supply is starting to get dangerously low and they do not know for sure how long that they can stretch it out. If they really try very hard, they figure that they might be able to make it last for one or two years longer. Three more months had gone by and the probes have not located a suitable planet yet. Nevertheless, the probes are scanning the entire areas that they have been sent to. So far, the planets are barren and lifeless. They think that at this time that they may be to far away from the sun yet. However, they are still not going to give up. For giving up is just not their way of nature. For their way of nature is to keep on trying, even if it takes them the rest of their lives to find the answer. Part of their continuous venture on trying was based on their way of life from earth. Not only was it bred into them, but also that it was their upbringing. They were taught from early childhood to never quit or give up. Mixing that with their Telaxian way of life really created a strong belief in never giving up. For the Telaxians were taught to search for another answer instead of giving up. That if they did give up, that it would cost them their entire life or even the lives of others. Therefore, their stride in life is that they should always seek an answer, even if it seems impossible.

CHAPTER *Six*

O ne month later, one of the probes had found something that might be what they have been searching for all of these years. This planet had gotten their hopes up very again. For this planet was only six more months away from their present position. From the information that they have received back from the probe, that this planet is a bluish one in color. To them this is a very good sign. The other information is that the probe has not detected any signs of life on the planet. That will even make this better for them. Because if this planet does have plenty of water on it, then that would definitely make a great home for them. Providing that the atmosphere is not poisonous to them all. They turned the mighty ship towards the direction that they probe has indicated. They only had to turn the ship by seven degrees to their left. This still kept them moving towards the sun. Nevertheless, on a more parallel course. It would take them three times longer to reach the sun on this course. They had started preparing for the possible planetary visit even though they are a few months away. They sent another probe to this planet. This one will enter the atmosphere and send back all the information that, they will need before they get there.

From the signals that they will receive from this probe, will enable them to see everything that they want to see on this planet. It will take approximately one month for the probe to reach the planet. They kept close contact with the probes journey towards the planet. The closer it got, the more anxious that they were. For they were very tired of being locked up inside of their ship. They longed for the real feel of natural sunlight on their skin, as well as the feel of natural water. They also wanted to see what the soil and rock felt like again. The ship was comfortable, but it was not their home.

Tylaxor had sent three messengers to the elder's ship to let them know that they have found a possible home world for them. It took the messengers two and a half hours to reach the ship. When they got there, they could not get in to talk with them. Then they tried to use the emergency telecom system to reach them. However, they received no answer back of any kind. They did not know if they were ignoring them or if something had actually happened to the elders. Because nobody knew how old he or she were at any given time. The elders just did not tell them. They went back to Tylaxor and told her what they had found out. They told her that they could not get any kind of answer out of them. She said that she would take a small group up there with her to find out what was wrong. She asked them if they tried to open the door with their handprints. They told her that they did, but it would not open for them. She said that they probably coded the receptacle for only a small few of them.

After two hours, they reached the door to the elder's ship again. Tylaxor put her hand on the receptor. The door opened right up for her. She said that they probably encoded her DNA into the system. Because she was one of the first to become just like them. Then they proceeded towards the control room where some of the elders should have been. However, when they got there, they found it empty. There was absolutely no one there. Nevertheless, there should have been at least one hundred of them here. She decided to look around the ship for them. Everywhere they looked, no one was there. She went back to the control room and turned on the message viewer. There she found out what had happened. The message stated that they were too old to make the complete trip to another planet. They said that they knew that she would find a new home for them all. Otherwise, she would not be seeing the memory transmission that they left behind. They said that died ten years back. They also said that she would not find any traces of them aboard the ship. Therefore, there is no use in looking around for them, for they had turned the ships automatic system on. This system would destroy any living thing that has recently stopped living. The other part of the message said that Tylaxor is the sole leader of the people, and that this was now her ship. She will in turn choose the ones that she sees fit to be on the mighty council.

The great council consists of four chapters. The first one will consist of eleven members. The second chapter of the council consists of nine members. The third chapter consists of six members, and the fourth chapter can only consist of three members. They said that they have chosen her .because of her feelings towards life. In addition, they said that they have been monitoring her during the short time that they had left to live. Moreover, they knew that she was the best choice, for she has final say over all of them. The message then said for them all to have a well life. Then the message ended.

Tylaxor knew what she must do. She made out a list of people that she wanted to see right away. She then handed the list to the one she named to be the Council Crier. His duty was to make all reports that the Council makes a public record. She then told him to push a series of six points on the console. This will broadcast all over the entire ship. He called the twenty-nine people that she has chosen to be on the Council. Then in the next five hours will make another statement over the system. Until that time, everyone is to return back to what they were doing.

Two hours after the message ended, the twenty-nine showed up at the elders ship where Tylaxor was waiting. She then told for all except those whom she has called to leave the room and seal the door. She then told them to have a seat at the Councils table. Among the twenty-nine members was her husband Truax. He has been given the most authority above the others. She told him that if he had any complaints about whom she has picked, for him to speak his peace. For if, he does not, that is the way that this will remain. He told her that she has made a very wise choice in those that she has chosen. Before she tells them, what chapters that they are in, the Council Crier will explain the message that was left for her. It took the Crier half an hour to tell them the entire message. They said that they understood why this was the way that it is.

Tylaxor said that the following ones were chosen to be in the first chapter are; John, Eric, Dale, General Hawser, Cornel Davis, Major Ann Frank, Major Tom Elliot, Captain Miller, Captain Johnson, Nancy Adams, And Ruth Coleman. The Second Chapter is; Earl Jones,

George Lumas, John Edwards, Mike Hendricks, Terry Saunders, Larry Potts, Jerry Stone, Peter Boils, and Sherry Dolder. The Third Chapter is; Henry Wilks, John Ericson, Mickey Manchez, Susanah Perrish, Connie Simons, and Marshall Peters. The Fourth Chapter is; Jason Platts, Mark Younger, and Lily Meyers.

These people will honor the elder's code of Dignity. Then she assigned them all except her husband a fleet of ships to command. Her husband will stay by her side and command them all. As the next five months went by, they had almost everything ready for a planetary visit. They received more information back from the probe. The planet does have a small portion of vegetation on certain parts of the land mass. The Planet is covered by three-fourths water. Only one quarter is dry land. This is a very suitable planet so far. Now they need to find out if the atmosphere is safe enough for them to breathe. If it is, then they will call this their home. The planet seems to have a large cloud mass all over it. The planet was also four times larger than what the Earth was. So to them, the land mass is about the same size as their real home planet. As far as locating any life signs on the planet, it turned up empty handed. For there were none to be found anywhere. The probe was given a signal to return to the ship with samples from the planet. The probe should return in about one or two weeks.

It took two weeks for the probe to return to the ship with samples from the planet. They checked the samples for every possible microbe that they knew about. So far it turned out to be safe for them. The air sample tested to be pure oxygen with the proper nitrogen particles that they needed to breathe. They had decided to land the entire ship onto the planets surface. Because this planet was so huge, that the ship would seem to be very small. Therefore, they will need all the power that they can get from the combined engines of all the crafts put together. The final preparations for the landing was completed. The ship was nearing the planet. They had reached the planet a whole week earlier than they thought. They brought the ship into the planets atmosphere and slowly down to the planet itself. It took them four hours to touch down on the soil of the land. They were not very far from the edge of the water. They made a few more tests before they decided to leave the ship.

Tylaxor wanted to make sure that the probe was not faulty with its information. If it turned out correct, then they will allow everyone to leave the ship and go where they wanted to go. Tylaxor said that before anyone goes anywhere, they must get the ship unloaded first. She said that she wanted the animals to be set free. Then the plants had to be brought out to be planted in the ground. Then the plankton had to be spread throughout the water so that it could grow. Or else they would not have any food at all.

Since there were enough people, she divided the work up into sections so that it all could be done at the same time. In the meantime, absolutely no one is to leave the ship until they finish all of the tests. They want to make sure that they will not die on this planet. She had them run some tests on the soil to see if it were hiding anything that might hurt them in any way. Then she wanted to run some tests on the water and find out what it has. Not only that, but they wanted to see what the sea life looks like out there.

They started unlinking the ships and lining them up along the bank of the water. Tylaxor went to one of the smaller ships and told them to lift off. They rose up off the ground and went towards the ocean. She told them to go out about twenty miles. Once they get there, they will submerge into the water and see what exactly is underneath the water. They reached the twenty-mile mark in about seven minutes after lift off. Then they dove into the water. What they were able to see was so astonishing. The sea creatures looked exactly like the ones that were on planet Earth that they had left behind years ago. They saw many types of fish. Including Whales, Dolphins, Swordfish, and Tuna. However, they could not find any sharks or other predators like them. This was completely unbelievable.

How did these sea creatures get here anyway? This was something that they were going to look into a bit more closely. She told the crew that they were going to stay down there for a while longer to investigate this water. They traveled about one hundred miles farther out to sea. They came upon a very large structure that looked similar to their own. However, the markings were a bit different. She was able to make out a little of what the markings said. The only three words that she could make out were, you are home. What was this suppose to mean? You are home. Was this message intended for them or was it meant for someone else? They circled the structure to see if there was any kind of entrance. Nevertheless, she could not see one. Then she saw something on the structure just above the sea floor. She new what that was for.

She told the pilot to move the ship within fifty feet of the circle. She then got up off her seat and went down to the transfer tube. She had them link it up to the side of the structure and drain out the water. Then they opened up the door and walked up to the wall. She put her hand on a mark that she knew quite well. A door opened up and they went in. They went up to the fifth level. Here everything looked all too familiar to them all. On this level was the nerve center for an entire city. She started placing her hands on the markings and turned on the power supply. Then she pressed a few more and the structure began to move, taking the ship with it. Half an hour later, the movement came to a halt. She turned on the view screen and saw the entire city right before her. She then pressed a few more of the symbols on the console. The movement started up again. However, this time they were going up. They saw the city begin to rise on the screen. It came to a complete stop after fifteen minutes. Half of the structures were sticking up out of the water. They looked like needles poking up out of the water. Then a message came on the screen. The message read. We knew that you would find this world if we pointed you in the right direction. This planet is now your new home. There will not be anyone to take it from you. We have brought the sea life here before. Now you have brought the plant and animal life. Take and plant the seeds and plant life into the soil and watch it blossom before your eyes. There are many new surprises here for you. Take good care of this world and it will take care of you.

> Hold this world in the palm of your hands,
> Treat it the way you would treat yourself,
> Let the waters flow through your veins,
> Like the blood moving through your heart.
>
> For you are with the lands,
> And trust what is on the shelf,

And take hold of the reins,
Leading them through the part.

While walking proud among the white sands,
Taking a strong hold on your wealth,
Leading those whom you train,
In addition, making them travel the path of your cart.

For if you place your heart upon the cart,
The sands will become the lands, Letting
their wealth become your stealth, Cherish
the land and it will cherish you.

This made a whole lot of sense to Tylaxor. For she knew what they were telling them. That was the end of the message that was left for them by their elders. She then knew that they had planned this all along. That is why they had made this trip once before. They are the ones responsible for bringing all of these different species of sea life to this planet. Their intentions must have been to create another planet similar to both types of beings. Their reasons for doing all of this must have been straight from the heart. She then pressed a few more of the symbols on the console and the huge metro-plex city finished rising to the surface. What she could see on the viewer was very beautiful. The entire city actually looked like it was floating on top of the water. However, it really was not at all. It was just sitting there, no longer moving.

They went back to the ship and landed by the others. She told the others over the radio that it was safe to leave their ships. That this was definitely their new home. They left the ship and went to speak with the rest of the people. Tylaxor got out the device that they use to talk with the ones whom are to far away to hear well. This device made it possible for them all to hear everything that was said. She then told them about the huge city that the elders had built and left behind for them to find. All that the elders did was to point them in the right direction. She said that they will remain on the land until all of the plants and animals are completely cared for. Alternatively, until they reach a point in time when they can care for themselves.

They ended up caring for the plants and animals for a period of two years. At the end of the two years, the population had grown three times the original size. Now Tylaxor and her people are able to go to their own city so that the plants and animals can have their own lives as well. Tylaxors people told the animals that they would come to visit them at least twice a week. This way the animals would never forget their true friends.

Every now and then, the Dolphins came to visit the ones who gave them a new lease on life. For they enjoy sharing the water with Tylaxor's people. They even give Tylaxor's people a ride and play with them.

CHAPTER *Seven*

Throughout the next few months, Tylaxor has spent numerous hours sifting through the memory banks in her personal database. She was searching for any information on what might happen to them in the future. She was looking for one thing in particular. She wanted to know what the outcome would be on their changes. So far, she has not been able to find even the smallest clue. Three days later, she stumbled onto a couple of closed files in her database. It took her fourteen hours to crack the code on the first one. However, when she did, she was very surprised. What she had discovered was a secret file that was left by her elders.

This file told her about many things. Including the reason for them being brought here. The two main reasons were; One - The two worlds were both on a self-destruction course. Two - The new world needed to be populated to survive. Then they came up with an idea to give both worlds a new lease on life by taking bits and pieces of each and combining them to make a single, but better being and world. They knew that there might be a few differences between the two types of beings. Nevertheless, they were rapidly approaching their time when they would eventually die. However, that is not what they wanted. They wanted someone to remember them someday in the future. This was the only way to do it.

The elder said in his file that they had become sterile and could no longer give birth to any newborns. However, they also knew that there was one way that was forbidden by their elders. That was to take another species to make theirs. They were told that this process could create mutants that might destroy everything or even everyone. Nevertheless, this was not going to stop them in their decision. They knew that their kind would not live much longer. So they went ahead with their plans to create a new race. The new beings will have increased brainpower and activity. Their heads would also grow beyond their normal size. Then their outer structure would also change, for they would eventually become a different type of human being. They would lose one set of eyes and their teeth would become more like they did when they were completely human. However, they would keep their webbed feet and the fin on their backs. Their skin tone would change to a more suitable color. Almost the same as when they were human. They also said that they may grow wings on their backs, but they were not sure of that one. And their mouths would grow to where they could eat fruit, vegetables, and some fish. That they will also stop feeding on plankton. They will retain their gills so that can breathe under water and still be able to breathe on land for days at a time. That they will no longer have the need to get their skin wet to survive.

The only problem that they would face is that they did not know how much more the new ones would develop. Alternatively, how much longer they would live. It was possible that they could only live two hundred years or even up to five hundred years or longer yet. It all depended on what kind of life they lived. If they lived the type of life that had been planned out for them, they could live for hundreds of years. She had finished reading the first secret file of her elders.

She then started working on the second file. This time it only took her one hour to crack the code, or she got the idea that it would be similar to the first one. In this file, she found out some interesting information about this planet. One thing that she found out was that there are three more of the underwater metro-plex's. They were all in different parts of the ocean. Not only that, but also each one is twice the size of the first one. In addition, there was several places in the ocean to put the ships in for storage. The message then said that there are detailed maps at the end of the file telling the locations of the other places.

Next, she found out that there is a massive portal in which they can travel back and forth to their home planet. That there is another portal near planet earth. The portal on this end is in orbit around the third moon for this planet. This was shocking to her. She wondered why they didn't use the portal to begin with. Maybe they wanted to see if she could handle being out in space for a long period. She really did not know. It also told her that there is a special symbol on her console that will operate the portal. Moreover, that it is only on her ship. No other ship can use the portal without the company of this one. She was glad that they thought of something like this. Now they can go back home and get more people and bring them back here. The end of the message came up and there before her were the maps to where everything was hidden. She quickly downloaded the maps into her database.

She finished the second file of her elders. She then input the information into her regular database and cross-referenced it with the other information that she already accumulated. She found out that they are living within the set parameters that was laid out for them. Also with this, she found out that they could expect to live beyond five hundred years. How much longer depended on their social structure in life itself. This really made her feel real good, for she thought that she would no longer live past the two hundred mark. Now that she has found out otherwise, she is totally a new person.

Now she and her husband Truax can have quite a few more newborns if they want to without having to worry about being sterile. Because that just will not happen for a few hundred years. She took the information to her council to see if they thought that she should tell the entire population about her discovery. On the other hand, if she should keep it a secret and let them find out on their own.

The Council met for about three and a half hours discussing the matter at hand. They suggested that they should tell them in order to prevent future disasters. For if, they find out that they can live even longer, that it might keep their heads on level ground. During the last half hour, they took a vote to determine the outcome of the information. It was a unanimous vote that everyone would be told of the discovery. In addition, all that goes with it. They got up from the table and went out to the main hall where the people were waiting for them. She picked up the device and told them of the new discovery that would benefit them, for their entire lives. She also told them that there were no clues as to how long they could actually live. However, there was one drawback. In order for them to live this extravagant life, they must continue on the course that had been set for them. She said that they had a right to know that they will live for quite a very long time. In addition, the real good part since they were going to live for a very long time and the huge size of the planet that they do not have to worry about over populating for several millenniums.

Tylaxor told them that she wanted a thousand volunteers to go with her in her ship to locate the other three cities. That she wanted to see exactly how much bigger they were so she could decide where to settle down. It took three hours for everyone to board the ship so that they could leave. On the map, it showed that one of the cities was only two hundred mile away. Therefore, they went there first. They found it at the depth of five hundred feet below the surface. She found the docking bay and entered it. It was dark and cool inside, probably from not being used. They located the main operations room. It was located on the fourth level of the complex. She started to press a series of buttons and the huge city began to rise to the surface. She then pressed a few more and the dark city started to light up. It took a whole hour for this one to reach the surface. Nevertheless, when it finally cam to a stop, it was awesome. She had left fifty people there to run things while she went to locate the next one.

This one was located on the other side of the planet and she knew that it would take her at least a whole day to get there. They decided to go ahead and get there as quickly as they could. On the next day, they found the city about one hundred and fifty miles from shore. It too was at the five hundred foot depth. They had no trouble raising this one to the surface. She left another fifty people behind to maintain the city. Then finally, they headed for the fourth one. It was two hundred miles south of the this one. It only took them half an hour to find it. They raised it to the surface and had turned on the lights. Fifty more people were left behind to take care of the city.

She then wanted to go check out the portal in space. They made sure that they had water and food aboard the ship before leaving the planet. They decided to use only one of the large holds for this. They did not want to take any chances out there. After three days of careful planning, they were ready to lift off. The mighty ship broke free of the planet and was on their way to the third moon. She was amazed at how many moons this planet actually had. They counted seven to be exact. The third moon seemed to be the largest of them all. Each one of these moons had a different orbit around the planet. They finally located the portal. It was enormous in size. They could fit the entire fleet of ships through it. However, they were only going to use this one for now. She pressed the button on her console and the portal began to open. They eased the ship into the portal and began to move through a wormhole. This wormhole shot them through very fast. They estimated that they were moving many times faster than the speed of light. How much faster, they could not tell.

After about six months of traveling through the wormhole, they came out on the other side. They ended up being in orbit around the moon from earth. This they liked much better. They could travel between Galaxies in such a short period. She told them to head back to earth and land in the northwestern part of the United States. After about two more days of space travel, they finally came upon the planet Earth. They landed in the state of Idaho. They picked this one because there were lots of open space that did not get to hot. The army met them. General Hawser met with them and explained that they were not aliens. He told them that they were originally from this planet. They of coarse didn't believe him. Therefore, he asked to see his friend General Mack Dillon. They wanted to know how he knew this person and he again told them that they were from this planet. Moreover, that he could prove everything that he told them. He under went his physical change and became human once again. The officers from the army could not believe what they were seeing. He then told them that Tylaxor was his leader now and that they need to peak with her, for she has great plans for this planet. They asked her to come out and talk with them. They wanted to know what kind of plans that she had for this planet. Tylaxor told them that all of the plans were of good in nature. That it will put an end to all of the wars and pollution. That they will go under one type of government. That they will no longer have a use for money any more. She told them that they will live a certain way only. She also told them that if they keep going in the direction that they are going, that they will eventually destroy the entire world.

This brought great concern to them all. Tylaxor then asked to speak with the people from the United Nations. She told them that only the leaders from all of the country's can decide for the fate of the world. That it must be a world decision. Nevertheless, she knows that not all of the people will agree to this. The ones that do will profit from it in the end. They told her that it would take a couple of days to a week to get them all together to meet with her. She said that would be fine with her, that she was in no hurry.

Five days later the world leaders finally met with Tylaxor. She again explained that the world was headed in self-destruction and that she could change their history altogether. She told them that she could make it to where they could live for hundreds of years. They also have space travel that they never knew about. That they will no longer need any type of money, which she could also put an end to the pollution and have nature take the land back. For the people would no longer need the land. That they would live in vast cities on the ocean and lakes. That they type of food would change and that they would much more knowledge than what they ever had. This of coarse was very over whelming for them all. They said that they would have to go back to their own countries and explain to their people about these new plans. They told her that it could take several months to get any kind of answer back. She said that she would wait for as long as it would take for their answer.

Tylaxor already had people lining up from the military wanting to undergo this new way of life. She told them that they have to wait for a spell until they build all of the machines that they will need to enhance their life span. She told them that there was no sense in building any machines until she knew that there were enough people to undergo the change. This they understood all to well. In addition, they did not want to push their luck with her.

It turned out that Tylaxor only had to wait for three days before she started to receive answers from the world. So far, four of the countries agreed to take the change. She had the military gather up all the materials needed for building the machines. She asked them if they minded building them in her ship. They asked her why. She told them that she did not want to clutter up the land with things that may never be used again. They understood and agreed that she was indeed right.

Over the period of the next six months, they had built over hundred thousand of the units. They had many crews working day and night to get it done as fast as they could.

She then told the people what changes they were going to take and how they will benefit from this. She told them that every two weeks they would let more people into the units. For that is how long the changes take. Then when they come out of the units, they will have to rest for at least six hours. In the meantime, she was telling those that did not want to undergo the changes, that they still can have a fruitful life. However, not here on the land. She also gave the governments the plans for building the vast cities out on the ocean. That these new cities will be their new homes. Once they are built, they will withstand any weather condition. She also said that they should put a stop to killing the animals on dry land. Cause they had a right to live too. She said that they could still harvest the fruits and berries with no fear from the animals. Because they would be told that, they will be safe and that they are not to harm anyone. So in the end, these people will be like care takers of the land. Getting it all cleaned up. She will see to it that they also get shuttles for transportation to and from the cities. Each of the cities will have at least fifty shuttles. That these shuttles emit no harmful fumes into the environment. They all agreed that this was also a suitable solution that Tylaxor has come up with.

The next few months went according as planned. Many thousands have under gone the new changes in life. They in turn where helping the others build the huge ocean cities. They had planned to build at least one hundred cities throughout the entire planet. That way there will be plenty of room for everyone. The people really enjoyed listening and talking with Tylaxor and her friends. They have learned so much since their arrival. By the end of a three-year period, Tylaxor had planned on turning over twenty million people into the new race of beings. She had told them about many new wonders that she had seen. This in turn intrigued the people much more and made some of them change their mind and they wanted to undergo the new change. Tylaxor did not hide anything from them. She wanted them to know as much as she does, for she is trying to save an entire world from destruction. However, she knows that she will not get them all.

The next thing that she had planned was for them to build vast ships for space travel and exploration. She said that this would help in discovering other planets that they can find to populate. She said that the universe is so large. Much larger than we ever thought of. She told them that she wanted to get things accomplished by the end of the third year. That she must eventually return to her new home planet that is much like this one here. Except that, one is clean and pure. They asked her about just space exploration. She told them that were part of the plan because she too wanted to see whatever life remains to be found. Nevertheless, she also said that would not happen until everything here is taken care of. She tried to answer all of their questions the best that she could.

Two of the three years has gone by and over thirteen million people had been changed. Much of the new cities were built. They were building the sections on the land and floating them out to the ocean. From their the sections were either sunk to fit other sections or connected to the side of a section. However, so far over fifty cities had been completely built and already inhabited. They also have built several ships and shuttles. She decided that all of the ships that were being built should be as large as hers for deep space exploration. For this would be the best way to go. People were everywhere working hard on getting everything done by the end of the next year. There was much to do and so little time left to do it in. The machines that were in her ship had been transferred to three of the other ships. She wanted this done this way in case she had to leave for home. In addition, this way they can keep changing people as time goes on. Because deep down inside, she knew that many more people were going to change there minds as they see their friends go away. Moreover, she really did not want to see anyone stranded here with nowhere to go.

The end of the third year was quickly ending. Tylaxor told them that she was going to leave and head back to her home planet. She told them where the portal was so they could come to her planet when they choose to. She also helped them form their own councils. She wanted them to have the best of everything. After making all of the necessary preparations, she had lifted off towards the portal for home. They made the six-month trip and found their planet once again. They landed on the planet and docked up with the city where she left the ship and went inside. She told the others that the trip was very successful. That she got millions of the people to undergo the new changes. She also told them to expect some of them to show up here.

From the progress that the planet was making, they knew that they had a home forever. They gave this planet the name of Ox. This name came from the way that the planet was thriving. It claimed the existence of all living creatures and helping them to survive. The planet willingly gave them all the nutrients that they desperately needed to stay alive and well. For this great quality, it was given a new name in its honor, which was called Ortatrox. In their native language, it meant, The Living Soul. For it was able to grow and prosper from knowledge and lots of love. This name came from the three planets that they were from, Earth, Telaxia, and the new one called Ox. Through the remainder of their lives, they will continue to teach the younger and make them understand to be kind and always love one another, for there may never be anyone else out there at all. Moreover, with these grand memories, Tylaxor takes Truax by his hand and together they pray that this planet will continue to help keep them all a thriving and thankful community. In addition, that this place that they have to live, is indeed, The Greatest Gift that they had ever received.

GLOSSARY

Trufolia (tru-fo-lia) A special vitamin that is essential for the infants sex and growth rate.

Telaxian Buggers (te-lax-ian buggers) which are really just a simple shuttlecraft

Pendomoses (pen-do-moses) these are tall structures that are called Pencil Domes.

Telaxian Alumini (te-lax-ian a-lu-mi-ni) this is a clear aluminum and steel alloy mixed with Plexiglas. It is stronger than any material know to humankind. It is also very thin and lightweight.

Ortatrox (Or-ta-trox) which means the living soul.

Tylaxor (Ty-Iax-or) means the leader of a nation.

Truax (tru-ax) means someone "With great authority and knowledge.

Mintok (Min-tok) means the brave one.

Tuluxor (To-lux-or) means the adventuring seeker.

Mytrox (My-trox) means the specialist.

Matrix (Ma-trix) means the mix master.

Mytroaterian (My-trox-a-ter-ian) means the queen of the flowers.

Trulaxator (Tru-Iax-a-tor) means the truth sayer.

Mytroxator (My-trox-a-tor) means the wild flower child.

Ox the hearty one that thrives well.

Yearling which is the first of four stages in the new life.

Signotin (Sig-no-tin) means dweller in time travel.

Bluton (Blu-ton) means the expediter.

Silvatar (Sil-va-tar) means the silent shinning star.

Printed in the United States
By Bookmasters